Rob pulled her
what she had b
days now, pres.
and kissing hin

He responded in kind, his lips claiming hers in a kiss that left her dizzy, heart pounding, craving more.

She pressed him back against the wall and began fumbling with the buttons of his shirt. Her fingers brushed at the hair on his chest and he growled against her throat, a shiver of pleasure running through her.

"Any other guests here?" he mumbled into her hair.

"No."

"Good." He slid his hands under her thighs and hoisted her up against him, and kissed her again. Her heart pounded so hard she imagined she could hear it.

Then she realized it wasn't her heart she was hearing—it was footsteps, pounding up the walk outside. She broke the kiss and pushed at Rob. "Someone—"

But it was the only word she managed before the front window broke and flames leaped across the room.

DANGER ON DAKOTA RIDGE

CINDI MYERS

If you purchased this book without a cover you should be aware that this book is stolen property. It was reported as "unsold and destroyed" to the publisher, and neither the author nor the publisher has received any payment for this "stripped book."

For Susan

ISBN-13: 978-1-335-52668-7

Danger on Dakota Ridge

Copyright © 2018 by Cynthia Myers

Recycling programs for this product may not exist in your area.

All rights reserved. Except for use in any review, the reproduction or utilization of this work in whole or in part in any form by any electronic, mechanical or other means, now known or hereafter invented, including xerography, photocopying and recording, or in any information storage or retrieval system, is forbidden without the written permission of the publisher, Harlequin Enterprises Limited, 22 Adelaide St. West, 40th Floor, Toronto, Ontario M5H 4E3, Canada.

This is a work of fiction. Names, characters, places and incidents are either the product of the author's imagination or are used fictitiously, and any resemblance to actual persons, living or dead, business establishments, events or locales is entirely coincidental.

This edition published by arrangement with Harlequin Books S.A.

For questions and comments about the quality of this book, please contact us at CustomerService@Harlequin.com.

® and TM are trademarks of Harlequin Enterprises Limited or its corporate affiliates. Trademarks indicated with ® are registered in the United States Patent and Trademark Office, the Canadian Intellectual Property Office and in other countries.

HARLEQUIN®
www.Harlequin.com

Printed in U.S.A.

Cindi Myers is the author of more than fifty novels. When she's not crafting new romance plots, she enjoys skiing, gardening, cooking, crafting and daydreaming. A lover of small-town life, she lives with her husband and two spoiled dogs in the Colorado mountains.

Books by Cindi Myers

Harlequin Intrigue

Eagle Mountain Murder Mystery

Saved by the Sheriff
Avalanche of Trouble
Deputy Defender
Danger on Dakota Ridge

The Ranger Brigade: Family Secrets

Murder in Black Canyon
Undercover Husband
Manhunt on Mystic Mesa
Soldier's Promise
Missing in Blue Mesa
Stranded with the Suspect

The Men of Search Team Seven

Colorado Crime Scene
Lawman on the Hunt
Christmas Kidnapping
PhD Protector

Visit the Author Profile page at Harlequin.com.

CAST OF CHARACTERS

Paige Riddell—Fiercely independent, unfailingly loyal, with clear ideas about right and wrong, Paige hides her insecurities behind a confrontational personality. She fights her attraction to the DEA agent she holds responsible for her brother's downfall, but she grows to depend on him when her life is threatened.

Agent Rob Allerton—The DEA agent has returned to Eagle Mountain to investigate the death of developer Henry Hake, but he hadn't planned on getting involved with his former adversary, Paige. Though they clashed when he arrested her younger brother, he's always been attracted to the fiery blonde.

Parker Riddell—After a stint in prison and rehab, Parker is getting his life together and helping Professor Val Gibson dig into the history of biological weapons development in the area during World War II. But Parker's impulsive nature may land him in trouble he can't get out of.

Professor Gibson—The eightysomething retired history professor is determined to discover the location of the government's secret World War II biological weapons laboratory.

Bryce Reed—The CFO of CNG Development, Bryce came to town to sell locals on CNG's plans to develop a research laboratory on property they own on Dakota Ridge.

Henry Hake—The real estate developer's death under mysterious circumstances has focused attention on the property he once owned on Dakota Ridge.

Larry Rowe—The mayor of Eagle Mountain is keen to have CNG's new development in the area. He's never one to miss a chance for the spotlight, and keeps a close eye on developments at the Dakota Ridge property.

Chapter One

What she was planning wasn't illegal, Paige Riddell told herself as she hiked up the trail to Dakota Ridge. Her friend Deputy Gage Walker might not agree, but she hadn't asked his opinion. The mayor of Eagle Mountain, Larry Rowe, would object, but Larry always took the side of corporations and businesses over people like Paige—especially Paige. But she knew she was right. CNG Development was the one breaking the law, and she had a copy of a court order in her pocket to prove it.

The tools she carried clanked as she made her way up the forest trail. She had borrowed the hacksaw from a neighbor, telling him she needed to cut up an old folding table to put out for recycling. The bolt cutters were new, purchased at a hardware store out of town. Planning for this expedition had been exciting, she had to admit—a nice break from her routine life of managing the Bear's Den Bed and Breakfast Inn and volunteering for various causes.

She stopped to catch her breath and readjust the straps on her pack. A chill breeze sent a swirl of dried aspen leaves across her path, bringing with it the scent of pine. In another week or two, snow would dust the top of Dakota Ridge, rising in the distance on her right. In another month, people would be taking to the trail with snowshoes instead of hiking boots. Thanks to Paige, they would be able to make their way all the way up and along the top of the ridge, their progress unimpeded by CNG's illegal gate.

She set out again, walking faster as she neared her destination, a mixture of nerves and excitement humming through her. She planned to leave the copy of the court order at the gate after she cut off the locks, so that whichever CNG employee discovered the damage would know this wasn't a random act of vandalism, but an effort to enforce the court's ruling that CNG couldn't block access to a public trail that had been in use across this land since the late nineteenth century.

The trail turned and followed alongside an eight-foot fence of welded iron and fine-mesh wire. Snarls of razor wire adorned the top of the fence. Paige was sure the razor wire hadn't been there when she had last hiked up this way about ten days ago. What was so important on the other side of that fence that CNG felt the need to protect it with razor wire?

She quickened her pace. CNG had the right to protect its property however it saw fit, but if the management wanted to keep out hikers, they needed to reroute their fence. Maybe wrecking their gate would encourage them to do so. Waiting for them to comply with the court ruling hadn't worked, so it was time for action.

She had considered asking other members of the Eagle Mountain Environmental Action Group to join her. The local hiking club, which had evolved into the closest thing Rayford County had to a political action committee, had a diverse membership of active people, most of whom were already up in arms about the gate over one of the most popular trails in the area. With more people and more tools, they probably could have dismantled the obstruction. But more people involved meant a greater chance of discovery. Someone would shoot off their mouth in a bar or to the wrong friend, and the next thing Paige knew, CNG would have filed a countersuit or criminal charges or something. Better to do this by herself—less chance of getting caught. CNG might suspect her of having something to do with the messed-up gate, since she was head of the EMEAG and one of its most vocal members, but they would never be able to prove it.

She quickened her pace as the offending gate came into view. Welded of black iron, four feet wide and at least six feet tall, topped with pointed spikes, it sported a massive padlock and the kind of chain Paige associated with cargo ships, each link easily three inches across. She stopped a few feet away, slipped the pack from her back and dropped it onto the ground beside the trail, where it settled with an audible *clank*.

She moved closer, inspecting the setup. The lock

was new, made of heavy brass. She had heard Gage had shot the old one off when he and his girlfriend, Maya, were up here searching for her missing niece. Paige grabbed the lock—which was bigger than her hand—and tugged. Not that she expected it to be open, but she would have felt really foolish if she went to the trouble to cut it off, then found out it hadn't even been fastened.

The lock weighed several pounds. The hasp was thick, too. She returned to her pack and fished out the cutters and the hacksaw. Some videos she had watched online had showed people slicing through locks with portable grinders, but that approach had struck her as noisy and likely to attract attention. Better to snip the lock off with the bolt cutters, or saw through the hasp.

She tried the bolt cutters first, gripping the hasp of the lock between the jaws of the cutters and bearing down with all her might.

Nothing. They didn't even make a dent in the metal. She gritted her teeth and tried again, grunting with the effort. Nothing, save for a faint scratch. A little out of breath, she straightened, scowling at the recalcitrant lock. Fine. Time to get the hacksaw. Her neighbor had assured her it would cut through metal.

Sawing the blade was hard, tiring work, but after half a dozen strong strokes, she had succeeded in making a dent in the hasp. Another half hour or so of work and she might sever the hasp—provided her arm didn't fall off first. But hey—she wasn't a quitter. She bore down and sawed faster.

She was concentrating so hard on the work she didn't hear the voices until they were almost on her. "Over here!" a man shouted, and Paige bit back a yelp and almost dropped the saw.

She recovered quickly, gathered her tools and raced into the underbrush, heart hammering painfully. She waited for the voices to come closer, for someone to notice the damage to the lock and complain. Had they seen her?

Her pack! Feeling sick to her stomach, she shifted her gaze to the dark blue backpack clearly visible by the side of the trail. Did she dare retrieve it? But moving would surely attract attention.

She held her breath as two men in forest camo parkas, watch caps pulled down low on their foreheads, emerged from the woods on CNG's side of the gate and tramped down the trail toward her. She shrank farther back into the underbrush, sharp thorns from wild roses catching on the nylon of her jacket and scratching the backs of her hands. Her eyes widened and her heart beat even faster as the men drew nearer and she could make out semiautomatic weapons slung across their backs. Since when did a real-estate development company equip their security guards with guns like that?

Talk about overkill! Anger took the place of some of her fear. If those big bullies thought they could intimidate her, they had another think coming. She had every right to be here, on a public trail, and if they didn't like it, they could take it up with the sheriff's department, but she was in the right.

She had about decided to emerge from her hiding place and tell them so when they reached the gate. But instead of stopping and opening it, or yelling out at her, the two men walked past, along the fence line. Now Paige could see they carried something between them. Something heavy, in a large wooden packing crate. She shuddered as they passed. Though the shape wasn't exactly right, the big box reminded her of a coffin. What the heck were these two doing with that out here in the middle of nowhere? After all, there was a perfectly good road leading right onto the property, which had once been planned as a luxury resort. Last she had heard, CNG wanted to turn the abandoned resort into a high-altitude research laboratory. So why sneak through the woods carrying a heavy box instead of just driving it to wherever they needed it? And why carry guns along with the box?

As soon as the men had passed her hiding place and moved out of sight, Paige emerged. She shoved the tools and the pack out of sight under some bearberry bushes, then hurried down the trail after the men. The former Eagle Mountain Resort had been the site of plenty of shady activity lately—maybe this was more of the same. It was her duty as a citizen to find out. Besides, who could resist a mystery like this?

She didn't have any trouble tracking the two men. They crashed through the underbrush like a pair of bull elk. They probably didn't expect anyone else to be up here. Word had gotten out around town that the trail was blocked, and no one lived on the abandoned mining claims that surrounded CNG's property, except Ed Roberts, who was practically a hermit and made a point of keeping to himself. Paige had counted on that same privacy to help her get away with cutting the lock off the gate. She'd have to make another attempt at that. Next time, she would bring more muscle, and maybe power tools.

Wherever the two guys with guns were headed, they weren't wasting any time. Paige had to trot to keep up with them. Fortunately, the trail paralleling the fence made movement easy, and her lightweight hiking boots made little noise on the soft ground. She stayed far enough behind that the men would have to turn all the way around to see her, but she could still keep them in her sights.

A few hundred yards from the gate, they turned away from the trail. Paige stopped and crouched down. She watched through an opening in the underbrush as they carried the box about fifty feet, then stopped and set down their burden. The man in the lead bent and felt for something in the drying grass. The sound of metal scraping against metal carried clearly in the still air. The man turned around, then descended into the ground. The second man shoved the box toward the spot where his companion had disappeared and tipped it up, then slid it in. Then he disappeared after it.

Paige straightened, her mind racing to solve this puzzle. She looked around, noting her surroundings. Gage and Maya had been trapped in an underground chamber on the resort property. Maya's niece,

Casey, had climbed out and run for help. That must be the same chamber where the two men had disappeared just now. What were they doing in there? What was in that box? And why did they have to carry it through the woods instead of driving it to the storage bunker that led to the chamber?

She would definitely be paying Maya and Gage a visit to find out their take on all this. Of course, she had no proof anything at all illegal was going on, but given the property's history, it might be worth watching. She turned and made her way back down the trail and collected her pack and tools. She checked the lock again, but all her efforts had barely marked it. She would have to come up with a better plan.

Shouldering the pack once more, she started back down the trail. She needed to get back to the B and B. She had a new guest checking in this afternoon. Some government worker, Robert Allen. His secretary had made the reservation, and the credit card information she had given Paige had checked out. He had reserved her best suite for a week, a real bonus, considering this was her slow time of year—past prime summer tourist season, too late for fall leaf-peepers and too early for the Thanksgiving and Christmas holidays.

These thoughts occupied her until she reached the spot where the two men had turned away from the fence. She couldn't resist taking another peek, to see if she could make out anything else distinctive about the site. She bent over and wormed her way into the opening in the undergrowth, a more difficult task while wearing the pack. But she managed to wedge herself in there and look through—just in time to see the second man join the first up top. He bent and slid whatever cover was over the opening back in place. Then both men started straight toward her.

Paige quickly backed out of her hiding place, fighting the branches that snagged on her clothing and tangled in her pack. She swatted a vine out of her way and a thorn pricked her thumb, a bead of bright red blood welling against her white flesh. The tools in her backpack clanged like out-of-tune wind chimes as she pushed her way back toward the trail.

"Hey!" a man yelled.

Something whistled through the air past her and struck a tree to her left, sending splinters flying. A second gunshot followed the first. Paige yelped and ran, heart racing and legs pumping. Those maniacs were shooting at her! You couldn't shoot at someone on a public trail! Gage was definitely going to hear about this.

They weren't shooting anymore. They probably couldn't get a clear view of her. The trail was downhill and Paige ran fast. The two men would have to fight through heavy underbrush and get over or around that fence to pursue her. She had left her car parked at the trailhead and she was sure she could get to it before they could.

Idiots! In what universe did they think they could get away with something like this? You could bet she would be filing charges. She'd call the papers, too. CNG would get plenty of bad publicity from this fiasco. And when the corporate lawyers came calling to apologize and persuade her to settle out of court, she'd use that leverage to have them remove that gate over the trail. In fact, she'd make sure they donated some of their high-value ridgetop property as a conservation easement. They would have to if they had any hope of recovering their precious reputation.

Buoyed by these plans, she jogged down the trail, head bent, watching for roots and other obstacles that might trip her up. She didn't see the big man in the dark coat who stepped out in front of her—didn't register his presence at all until she crashed into him and his arms wrapped around her, holding her tight.

Chapter Two

As a DEA agent for the past fifteen years, Rob Allerton had faced down his share of men and women who wanted to kill him, but none had outright tried to run him over. The sound of gunfire had sent him charging up the trail, only to be almost mowed down by a female hiker who fought like a tornado when he grabbed hold of her to steady them both. He managed to pin her on the ground, then satisfied himself that she wasn't armed—and therefore probably not the source of the shots he had heard.

"I'm not going to hurt you," he said, speaking slowly and distinctly in her ear, ignoring the alluring floral fragrance that rose from the soft skin of her neck. "I'm a law enforcement officer. I only want to help." Carefully, he eased back and released his hold on her.

She sat up and swept a fall of straight honey-blond hair out of her eyes, and he felt the angry look she lasered at him in the pit of his stomach—and farther south, to tell the truth. He hadn't seen Paige Riddell in almost two years, but she wasn't the kind of woman a man forgot easily.

"Agent Allerton." She pronounced his name as if it was a particularly distasteful disease. He had figured out the first day they met that she seldom bothered masking her feelings or suppressing her passions. Feeling the heat of her hatred only made him wonder what it would be like to be on the receiving end of her love.

"What are you doing here?" she demanded, standing and dusting dirt from the knees of her jeans.

He rose also. "I heard gunshots. Was someone shooting at you?"

"*I* certainly wasn't shooting at *them*." She adjusted her pack, which clanked as she shifted her weight.

He frowned at the dark blue backpack. "Is that a *saw* you're carrying?" He walked around her to get a better look. "And a pair of bolt cutters?" He moved back in front of her. "What have you been up to?"

"None of your business." She tried to walk past him, but he blocked her way. She glared up at him, with those clear gray eyes that still had the power to mesmerize.

"It's my business if someone was shooting at you." He touched her upper arm, wary of startling her. "Are you okay? Are you hurt?" He should have asked the questions earlier, but he was so surprised to find her here he had forgotten himself.

"I'm fine." She shrugged off his hand, but he recognized the pallor beneath her tan.

"Who fired those shots?" he asked. "It sounded like a semiautomatic."

She glanced over her shoulder, in the direction she had run from. "I'm not going to stand here, waiting for them to come back," she said. "If you want to talk, you can come with me."

He let her move past him this time, and fell into step just behind her on the narrow trail. "Did you get a look at the shooters?" he asked. "Was it anyone you know?"

"I don't know who they were—two men up at the old Eagle Mountain Resort." She gestured toward the property to their left. The trail had turned away from the fence line and descended away from the property. "I spotted them carrying a big wooden crate through the woods. They lowered it into an underground chamber of some kind. At least, they both disappeared through some kind of trapdoor in the ground, and came out without the crate. I guess they saw me watching and fired. I took off running. They were on the other side of that big fence, so they couldn't chase me."

"Maybe they thought you were trying to break in," he said. "Were you using those bolt cutters on their fence?" He wished he could see her face, but she didn't look at him, and walked fast enough so that he had to work to keep up with her.

"No, I was not trying to break through their fence," she said.

"What were you doing? Bolt cutters and a saw aren't typical hiking gear."

"I was going to cut the illegal lock off their illegal gate over a legal public hiking trail," she said. "I have a copy of a court order instructing them to remove the lock and open the gate, which they haven't done."

"So you decided to take matters into your own hands," he said.

"The lock was too tough," she said. "I'll have to get someone up here with power tools or a torch or something." She might have been discussing her plans to build a community playground or something equally as virtuous. Then again, Paige Riddell probably saw opening up a public trail as just as worthy an enterprise. This was the Paige he remembered, absolutely certain in her definitions of right and wrong, and that she, of course, was in the right.

"You're not worried someone is going to shoot at you again?" he asked. "Next time they might not miss."

She glanced back at him. "I'm going to report this to the sheriff. I was on a public trail. They had no right to fire on me. Even if I'd been trespassing— which I was not—they had no right to try to shoot me."

"You aren't the first person who's been fired on up here," Rob said. "Someone tried to shoot the sheriff and his deputies when they visited the property months ago."

"So there's a pattern of unlawful behavior," she said. "It's time to put a stop to it."

"Except no one can ever identify the shooters," Rob said.

"I could identify these men." She bent to duck under a low-hanging branch, then glanced back once more. "What are you doing here?" she asked. "I doubt you just decided it was a nice day for a hike."

"I'm staying in town for a few days—a little vacation time." Long practice made him reluctant to share his plans with anyone, especially a woman he didn't know that well, who had made no secret of her dislike of him. "I heard a new company had taken over this property and I wanted to check out what they were doing here."

"You didn't find anything illegal when you were there last month, did you?" she asked.

"No." He had overseen an investigation into an underground laboratory that had been discovered on the property, but his team had found no signs of illegal activity.

"The new owners say they're going to use the property to build a high-altitude research facility," she said. "Did you know that?"

"I heard something to that effect," he said. "What do you think of that idea?" Paige headed up the local environmental group that had gotten the injunction that stopped development at the resort years ago.

"It's better than a resort that only gets used half the year," she said. "Depending on what they research, that kind of facility might actually do some good, and I wouldn't expect a lot of traffic or other stressors on the environment. We'll wait and see what they plan to do, and we'll definitely have some of our members at their permit hearings."

"Do you ever worry you'll get on the wrong side of the wrong person?" he asked.

She stopped so suddenly he almost collided with her. She turned to face him. "No, I'm not afraid," she said. "The kinds of people we do battle with—people or companies who want to do harmful things for their own gain, without thought for others—they want us to be afraid. They count on it, even. I'm not going to give them that satisfaction." She turned and started walking again.

"You don't think that's foolhardy sometimes?" he asked, picking up his pace and squeezing in beside her. "Not everyone plays by the rules. Some of them can be downright nasty." He had met his share of the second type in his years in drug enforcement.

"I try to be smart and careful, but I'm not going to back down when I'm in the right."

There was that passion again, practically sparking from her eyes. He couldn't help but admire that about her, even when they had been sparring on opposite sides of a battle. "Tell the sheriff what you saw," he said. "Then let him and his deputies handle this. Don't go up there by yourself again."

"I told you I try to be smart," she said. "Next time I'll go up there with other people. I might even have a reporter with me." She smiled. "Yes, I think that would be a great idea. Companies like CNG hate bad publicity."

They reached the trailhead, where his black pickup truck was parked beside her red Prius. She studied the truck. "Is that yours?" she asked.

"Yes. It's my personal vehicle. I told you, I'm on vacation."

She turned to him again. "I just realized I've never seen you when you weren't wearing a suit." Her gaze swept over his hiking boots and jeans, over the blue plaid flannel shirt, up to his hair, which he hadn't found time to get cut lately. He felt self-conscious under that piercing gaze, wondering if he measured up. Did Paige like what she saw? Was he vain, hoping the answer was yes?

But her expression was impossible to decipher. He half expected her to say something derogatory, or at least mocking. Instead, she said, "I guess the truck suits you."

What was that supposed to mean? But before he could ask her, she stashed the pack in the back seat of the Prius, climbed into the driver's seat and sped away, leaving him standing beside his truck, feeling that, once again, Paige had gotten the upper hand.

Of the people she might have expected to encounter on the trail that morning, Paige had to admit that DEA agent Rob Allerton was probably five hundredth on the list of possibilities. Sure, he had ended up in Eagle Mountain a month ago, leading an investigation into that underground lab, but she had managed to avoid crossing paths with him. Once he had wrapped that up and gone back to live and work in Denver, she had comforted herself that she would never have to see the man again.

Now that she was alone, and the full impact of

what had happened up on Dakota Ridge was making her break out in a cold sweat, she could admit that she had been relieved to see him, once she realized he wasn't a friend of the shooters. Rob Allerton might be a coldhearted pain in the behind, but he had probably been armed, and he knew how to handle criminals. For all her talk of not letting fear make her back down, she had been relieved not to have to face those two men and their guns by herself.

She gripped the steering wheel more tightly and glanced in the rearview mirror, to see Rob's Ford pickup behind her. She might have known he would drive a truck. He had always had a bit of a cowboy swagger—something she might have admired if they hadn't been adversaries.

And they were adversaries, she reminded herself. Rob Allerton was the reason her brother, Parker, had ended up in jail, instead of in a rehab program where he belonged. She had fought like a mama bear—and spent most of her savings—to get her little brother into a program that would help him, and to get the sentence deferred if he completed all the requirements of his parole. Allerton hadn't lifted a finger to help her, and had in fact spoken out against any leniency for Parker. She was never going to forgive him for that.

Remembering how she had won that battle, and that Parker was all right now and well on his way to putting his life back together, calmed her. She rubbed her shoulder, where it ached from carrying the pack and tools, and slid her hand around to massage the back of her neck, then froze. Her fingers groped around her collar, then back to the front of her throat, under her T-shirt. Her necklace was gone—the thin gold chain from which hung the gold charm of a bird in flight. She had purchased the necklace shortly after her divorce, as a symbol that she was free as a bird. She never took it off—but it was gone now. She swore to herself. The chain must have caught in the bushes when she pushed through them to get a better look at those two men. Or maybe when she had retreated.

She would have to go back up there later and look for it. But she wouldn't go alone. She would take plenty of friends with her, and she would make sure they were armed with more than bolt cutters and saws.

By the time she parked the Prius in front of the Rayford County Sheriff's Department, she felt ready to relate her story calmly. She headed up the walkway, only to meet Rob Allerton at the front door.

He held the door open for her. "After you."

"Are you following me?" she asked.

"I needed to check in with the sheriff anyway," he said.

"Why? I thought you said you were here on vacation."

"Just professional courtesy, to let him know I'm in town." He followed her into the reception area. "Besides, I can add my account of the shooting to yours."

"Agent Allerton! What a nice surprise!" Adelaide Kinkaid, the sixtysomething administrator for the sheriff's department, greeted Rob with a wide smile. She didn't exactly flutter her eyelashes at him, but the implication was there.

"Ms. Kinkaid. Nice to see you again." Rob clasped her hand and flashed a smile of his own, and Adelaide looked as if she might swoon. Paige crossed her arms over her chest and looked away. Honestly! It wasn't as if Rob Allerton was the only good-looking man on the planet. Yes, he had that young Jake Gyllenhaal charm going on that probably appealed to Adelaide's generation, but Paige had always liked men who were a little rougher around the edges. Less glib. Less deceptive.

"I just stopped by to say hello to the sheriff," Rob said. "Ms. Riddell needs to make a report of an incident up on Dakota Ridge, though."

"Oh, hello, Paige," Adelaide said. "I didn't see you standing there."

"No, I don't imagine you did," Paige muttered.

"Did you say an incident? On Dakota Ridge?" Sheriff Travis Walker, Gage's brother, joined them in the reception area. Clean-shaven and spit polished, Travis could have been a law enforcement poster boy. The fact that he was smarter than most and full of grit had made him a local hero, and at twenty-nine, the youngest sheriff in Rayford County history.

"It's Paige's story to tell," Rob said. "I only happened upon the tail end of things."

"Come into my office." Travis led them down the hall to his office and shut the door behind them. Paige sat in the chair in front of the battered wooden desk, while Travis took the black leather chair behind it. Rob stationed himself by the door. "Tell me what happened," Travis said.

"I hiked up the Dakota Ridge Trail this morning," Paige said. "I wanted to see if CNG Development had complied with the court order to remove the gate over the trail. They hadn't."

She glanced at Rob, daring him to reveal her plans to remove the lock, but he said nothing. "While I was up there, I saw two men on the other side of the gate, on the old Eagle Mountain Resort property. They didn't see me. They were carrying a large wooden crate between them—about the size of a coffin, though I don't think it was a coffin. It looked heavy. I thought it was really odd that they would be carrying something like that through the woods, instead of driving up to wherever they needed to be. The second thing that was odd was that both of the men had semiautomatic rifles slung over their backs. I'm no expert, but I think they were AR-15s."

Travis's brow wrinkled, and he pulled a pad of paper toward him and began making notes. "Can you describe these men?"

"Muscular—big shoulders. They were wearing forest camo parkas and black knit watch caps. I didn't get a really good look at their faces through the trees, but I didn't recognize them."

"What happened next?" Travis asked.

"They continued through the woods, on the other side of the fence. I went back down the trail, but I was curious to know what they were up to, so I followed them. They stopped and one of them bent down and

I heard the scrape of metal on metal. I think they opened a trapdoor or something. Then one of them climbed down into the ground. The other one pushed the box in and climbed down after it."

"So they went underground?" Travis asked. "Out of sight?"

She nodded. "I wondered if they were going into that same chamber where Gage and Maya were trapped this summer. But then I wondered again why they hadn't just driven up to it. Isn't it connected to that underground lab you found?" She looked to Rob for confirmation. "That's what Maya told me."

"It is," Rob said. "But we didn't find any sign that that chamber had been used for anything in a long time."

"That chamber is farther from the fence line," Travis said. "I don't think you could see the opening at the top from the fence."

"I don't think so, either," Rob said.

"Maybe it's just underground storage of some kind," Travis said.

"Fine, but why sneak through the woods, especially carrying something heavy?" she asked. "And why were those guys armed? And why did they shoot at me when they saw me watching them?"

"Did they say anything?" Travis asked.

"No. They just yelled 'Hey!' or something like that, and started firing. I couldn't get out of there fast enough."

"Did they try to follow you?" Travis asked.

"I don't know. I just ran." Her heart raced, remembering. "I knew they were on the other side of the fence and they'd have a hard time catching up to me. I figured I could make it to my car before they did. Then I ran into Agent Allerton." No sense elaborating on how he had pinned her to the ground. Though she had to admit that was after she did her best to knee him in the crotch.

"I heard the gunshots and came running up the trail," Rob said. "I met Paige coming down."

"What were you doing up there?" Travis asked.

Paige watched his face, not hiding her curiosity. Would he give the sheriff his story about a vacation? He shifted his weight. "I took some personal time to do a favor for my aunt."

"What kind of favor?" Travis asked.

Rob glanced at Paige. Was he going to ask her to leave the room, or suggest that he and Travis talk later? "I didn't ask you to leave while I told my story," she said. "I think I can hear yours."

"It's not exactly a secret," he said. "My aunt by marriage is Henry Hake's older sister. She asked me to look into his death a little more, see what I could find out."

"We're still investigating Henry Hake's death," Travis said. The man behind the Eagle Mountain Resort development had disappeared earlier in the summer. His body had been discovered on the property last month, but so far no one had been able to determine either how he had died or why.

"I'm not trying to step on any toes," Rob said. "But she's been worried sick since Hake disappeared early this summer. When he was found dead in that bunker on what had been his own property, it left her with more questions than answers. I told her I didn't expect to find anything you hadn't already learned, but she begged me to try." He shrugged. "I had some time off coming, and it's not exactly a hardship to spend a few days hanging around Eagle Mountain."

"Does your aunt have any ideas about what might have happened to her brother?" Travis asked.

"He had heart trouble, but she doesn't think he died of a heart attack," Rob said. "She's sure he was murdered. He was definitely afraid of someone in the weeks before he died. I'd like to find out who."

Chapter Three

Rob gave Travis credit—the sheriff didn't even blink when he learned Rob's reason for a return to Eagle Mountain. Paige, however, was gaping at him as if he had revealed a secret identity as a circus clown. "You're related to Henry Hake?" she asked.

"Not exactly," he said. "My uncle's second wife is Hake's sister. I never met the man." He turned to Travis. "And it's not my intention to interfere with your investigation. I just promised my aunt I would see what I could find out. I hiked up that trail this morning thinking I would start by getting another look at the place where his body was found—or as close as I could get, since the gates to the compound were locked up."

Travis nodded and turned back to Paige. "I'll go up to the resort property and take a look around. Do you think you could identify either of the men who shot at you if you saw them again?"

"Yes," she said.

"Good. I'll be in touch." He stood, and Paige rose also.

"While you're up there, would you look for my necklace?" she asked. "It's a gold chain, with a charm of a bird in flight. I was wearing it this morning and I don't have it now. I think it must have snagged on the bushes near where I was watching those two men."

"Sure, we can look for it," Travis said.

"Thank you, Sheriff," she said, and turned toward the door.

"Paige?"

"Yes, Sheriff?"

"Don't go up there by yourself anymore," Travis said. "At least until we get this settled. And tell the other hikers you know the same."

"All right." She turned toward Rob and acted as if she wanted to say something, then closed her mouth and left the room.

"Stay a minute," Travis said to Rob.

He nodded, and waited until they heard the front door close behind Paige before he took the seat she had vacated.

"Did you see either of the men she described?" Travis asked.

"No. I wasn't that far up the trail before she came barreling down." He chuckled. "I didn't recognize her at first, and I'm sure she didn't recognize me. When I took hold of her to try to calm her down, she fought like a tiger." He rubbed the side of his face, where she had scratched him.

"You knew each other before?" Travis asked.

Rob nodded. "Yes. And it's safe to say I am not one of her favorite people."

Travis waited, silent. He was probably a good interrogator, using silence to his benefit. "I'm the one who arrested her brother," Rob said.

"For possession of meth?" Travis asked.

"Yes. And for trying to sell stolen property. He was part of a group of addicts who were robbing apartment complexes in Denver. I was part of a joint drug task force working that case. We had already determined the thefts were linked to drugs."

"There was no doubt of his guilt?"

"None." He sighed, all the frustration of those days coming back to him. "Paige wanted an adjudicated sentence, with her brother, Parker, allowed to go to rehab instead of prison. I didn't agree."

"From what I've seen, she can be a little protective of Parker," Travis said.

"I get it. As far as I know, he's the only family she has. But the fact that part of my job was to help see that he was punished for his crimes made me the enemy. Her opinions about right and wrong tend to be very black-and-white."

"She went up there today to cut off that lock, didn't she?" Travis asked.

Rob grinned. "I didn't see a thing. Though she was carrying a hacksaw and a pair of bolt cutters with her."

Travis shook his head. "When Paige believes she's in the right, there's no changing her mind."

"I certainly learned that." Though he would have preferred she didn't see him as the bad guy. Still, she wasn't his chief concern at the moment. "As long as

I'm here, maybe I could help you out with Henry Hake's case," he said. "Is there anything you'd like me to look into? Unofficially, of course."

"Did your aunt say who her brother was afraid of?"

"No. Except she thinks it had something to do with his business."

"So not necessarily Eagle Mountain Resort. He had other real-estate holdings, didn't he?"

"A few apartment complexes and some office buildings," Rob said. "Eagle Mountain Resort was definitely his most ambitious project. When the court ordered him to stop development, I gather it put him in a financial bind."

Travis nodded. "That's what I've learned, also."

"What can you tell me about the property's new owners—CNG Development?" Rob asked.

"They're another real-estate development company, out of Utah. They're much larger than Hake Development, with projects all over the United States. I wondered why they even bothered with Hake—he was pretty small potatoes, compared to them."

"Maybe they're one of these companies that specializes in finding small firms in financial straits and buying them for bargain prices," Rob said.

"Maybe so."

"Paige says they want to build a research facility up there."

"So they've said. They haven't presented anything concrete to the town for approval. The couple of times

I've been up there since Hake's body was found, the place has been deserted."

"It wasn't deserted today," Rob said. "I'd sure like to know why those two were going around armed—and what was in that box. And why they reacted the way they did when they caught Paige watching them."

"Want to go up there with me to check it out?" Travis asked.

"You know I'm not officially on duty," Rob said. "My boss doesn't even know where I am."

"You wouldn't be participating in any official capacity," Travis said. "I just want someone to watch my back."

"I can do that." And maybe he would get lucky and discover something he could tell his aunt. He couldn't bring her brother back to her, but finding out what had really happened to him might ease her suffering a little bit.

THOUGH PAIGE VOWED to put Rob Allerton firmly out of her mind and focus on work at the bed-and-breakfast where she both lived and worked, she couldn't stop thinking about the man. He was always so aggravatingly calm and sure of himself. Having him here in town annoyed her, like walking around with a pebble in her shoe. Those days following Parker's arrest had been among the worst in recent memory. Her brother had needed help and men like Rob were preventing her from helping him. Yes, Parker had broken the law, but he wasn't a bad person. His addiction had led him to do things he never would have done otherwise. Instead of punishing him, why not treat his addiction and give him another chance?

Rob Allerton had made it clear he didn't believe in second chances. No thanks to him, Parker had at least gotten a chance to get clean, though he had had to serve time, too. But he was clean now, going to school and staying out of trouble. Another year and the charges would be wiped from his record.

But he was in that position only because Paige had fought for him. Other people weren't so lucky. They had to deal with the Rob Allertons of the world without anyone on their side.

She sat down at her desk off the kitchen and tried to put Rob out of her mind. His vacation wouldn't last forever, and she had more than enough to keep her occupied in the meantime. She was working there a little later when the back door opened and Parker entered. He dropped his backpack on the bench by the door and pushed his sunglasses on top of his head. To some of the more conservative people here in Eagle Mountain, he probably looked like trouble, with his full-sleeve tattoos and often sullen expression. But Paige saw past all that to the little boy she had read stories to and made macaroni and cheese for more times than she could remember. "How was class?" she asked.

"Okay." He opened the refrigerator. "What did you do today?"

Attempted vandalism and ended up getting shot at

by two thugs, she thought. "I was up on the Dakota Ridge Trail and you'll never guess who I ran into."

He took out a block of cheese and a plate of left-over ham. "I don't have to guess," he said. "You always tell me anyway."

"Rob Allerton is in town."

"Who?" He took a loaf of bread from the box on the counter and began making a sandwich.

"Rob Allerton. Agent Allerton? The DEA guy who arrested you?"

"What's he doing here?"

"He says he's on vacation." He hadn't told the sheriff about her attempt to cut the lock from the gate up on the trail, so she figured she could keep quiet about Rob's aunt and Henry Hake. Parker wouldn't care about any of that anyway.

"Maybe he wanted to see you," Parker said.

"Me?" She blew out a breath. "I'm sure I'm the last person he would ever want to see. Don't you remember how we clashed at your trial?"

"I remember sparks." He shot her a sideways look. "He thought you were hot."

"He did not!"

"You thought he was hot, too."

"You're delusional."

He turned back to his sandwich. "I'm not the one blushing."

"I'm not blushing. This room is too warm." She opened the refrigerator and began putting away the items he had removed. "Are you volunteering at the museum this afternoon?" she asked. She had talked

Parker into volunteering at the local history museum. Her friend Brenda Stenson, who ran the museum, needed the help, and it was a good way for Parker to keep busy. Everything she had read had said that having too much free time could be a problem for a recovering addict.

"No." He took a bite of the sandwich.

Paige tore off a paper towel and handed it to him. "What time does your shift at Peggy's start?" She had found him the job as a delivery driver at Peggy's Pizza as another way to keep him out of trouble.

"I'm off tonight," he said, then took another bite of sandwich.

"Oh. Well, I guess you can use the time to study." He was enrolled in classes at a nearby community college. Another condition of his parole.

"I'm going out," he said.

"With who?"

"A friend."

"Do I know this friend?"

"I doubt it."

"Parker, we are not going to do this."

"Do what?" He didn't bother trying to look innocent. If anything, he was annoyed.

"Don't make me give you the third degree," she said. "Just tell me who you're going out with. I don't think that's too much to ask."

"And it's not too much for me to ask that you give me a little privacy."

A flood of words came to mind, beginning with the notion that he had violated his right to privacy when he had gotten hooked on drugs, broken the law and gone to prison. But she had vowed when she took him in that she wasn't going to throw his mistakes back in his face. Her husband had done that and she knew how miserable and degraded it made her feel. So she swallowed back most of what she wanted to say.

"Be careful, and be quiet when you come in," she said.

"I will." Carrying the rest of his sandwich, he retreated to his room off the kitchen. Paige sagged against the counter. She was exhausted and it wasn't even one o'clock yet. Big guys with guns, Rob Allerton and her troublesome baby brother—maybe what she really needed was a vacation from men.

WHEN ROB AND TRAVIS arrived at the entrance to the former Eagle Mountain Resort, Rob wasn't surprised to find the gates shut tight. "This is how they were this morning when I stopped here," he said. He peered through the iron bars at what had once been the resort's main street. Weeds sprouted in holes in the asphalt, and in places the paving had disappeared altogether, the road little more than a gravel wash. A weathered sign still proclaimed that this was the future site of Eagle Mountain Resort, a Luxury Property from Hake Development. No sign of luxury remained in the crumbling foundations and sun-bleached wood of the few structures scattered about the property. Rocks ranging from those the size of a man's head to boulders as big as small cars spilled down from the ridge above at the site of a major rock slide where two men had been killed earlier in the year.

"It doesn't look any different than it did when I was here a month ago," Rob said.

"I'm guessing if CNG does plan to develop the place—for a research facility or anything else— they'll wait until spring," Travis said. "In another few months there will be eight to ten feet of snow up here. The county doesn't plow the road up this far and there's always a danger of avalanches on the ridge. It's one reason the judge agreed with Paige's group that a housing development up here was a bad idea."

Rob looked again at the deserted street. "What do we do now?" he asked.

"Let's hike up the trail a ways," Travis said. "You can show me where you were when you heard the shots, and where you ran into Paige."

They drove back down the road to the public trailhead, then started hiking uphill. After about half a mile, the trail began to parallel the fence line for CNG's property. The black iron fence, eight feet tall and topped with curls of razor wire, was almost hidden in places by a thick growth of wild roses and scrub oak, but in other spots the undergrowth thinned enough to provide a glimpse through the bars of the fence.

"About this point is where I heard the shots," Rob said. "I thought they came from the other side of the fence. I picked up speed and I hadn't gone far when

I saw Paige running down the trail toward me. I thought at first someone was pursuing her, but then I realized she was alone. She said two men had shot at her. Then my focus became getting her safely away."

"Did you stop by the entrance to the property before you went to the trailhead, the way we did just now?" Travis asked.

"Yes. The gates were locked and I didn't see anyone. No cars or anything."

"Let's see if we can figure out where Paige could have seen the shooters," Travis said.

They moved up the trail, which soon curved sharply, still following the fence line. Another hundred feet and they came to an opening in the wall of bushes and vines next to the trail. Broken branches and scuffs in the leaf litter told the tale of someone plunging into this opening—and exiting in a hurry.

Travis went first, with Rob close behind. Bending over, they had a clear view onto the resort property, but what they saw was unremarkable—a few stunted evergreens, oak brush with the last brown leaves of summer clinging to it, and some dried grasses. Travis took binoculars from his belt and scanned the area. "I don't see anything," he said.

They waited a moment, listening, but heard only the sound of their own breathing. The silence and the deserted—abandoned, really—property made Rob feel uneasy. "I don't think we're going to find anything here today," he said, keeping his voice low.

"No." They returned to the trail and started back toward the parking area. "I could try for a warrant to search the place," Travis said. "But I doubt a judge would grant the request."

"They were shooting at an unarmed woman," Rob said. "A woman who wasn't even on their property."

"That's what Paige said happened, but she wasn't hit and there weren't any witnesses."

Rob started to object, but Travis cut him off. "I know—it's not like her to make things up. I'm just telling you what CNG's lawyers are going to say."

"I heard the shots," Rob said.

"Right. People shoot guns all the time out here—at targets, at animals. It's elk season right now. Maybe they were hunting. It's not illegal to shoot off a gun."

Rob blew out a sigh of frustration. "So what do we do now?"

"We keep an eye on the place and look for a reason—any reason—to come back up here and take a closer look."

They fell silent, trudging down the trail. The sun was already disappearing behind the ridge, a chill descending in the fading light. Rob shoved his hands in the pockets of his jeans and reviewed the events of the morning in his head. Had he missed something—some clue that would help them figure out what was really going on? Had Paige's presence distracted him from noticing everything he should have noticed?

They reached the parking lot and Travis's SUV. The sheriff pulled out his keys and pressed the button to unlock the vehicle, but he froze in the act of reaching for the door handle, his gaze fixed on the door.

"What is it?" Rob, who had already opened the passenger door, asked.

"Take a look."

Rob walked around to the driver's side and stared at the thin gold chain affixed over the door handle with a piece of clear tape. A gold charm shaped like a bird dangled from the chain, stirred by a slight breeze. The sight of the delicate, feminine ornament so out of place sent a chill through him. "That looks like the necklace Paige described," he said. "The one she said she lost up here."

Chapter Four

Travis took out his phone and snapped several pictures of the necklace, then examined the ground around the vehicle. "This gravel is too hard-packed to leave prints," he said.

"We might get prints off the tape," Rob said.

Travis went to the back of the vehicle and opened it, then took out a small box. He put on gloves, then took out a paper evidence pouch and a thin-bladed knife. Carefully, he lifted the edge of the tape with the knife, then peeled it back. He transferred both tape and necklace to a plain white card, then slipped them in the pouch and labeled it. "I'll have a crime scene tech go over the car when we get back to the office," he said. "Though I doubt we're going to find much."

They both took another look around. Rob scanned the trees that surrounded the parking area. "Do you think they're watching us now?" he asked.

"The person or persons who put that necklace there?" Travis asked. He opened the door and slid into the driver's seat. "Maybe. Maybe they've been watching us the whole time."

"Why did they bother returning the necklace?" Rob asked, as he buckled his seat belt and Travis started the SUV.

"Maybe a hiker came along behind us, found the necklace on the trail and figured it must belong to whoever was in this vehicle," Travis said. "Or they figured giving it to a cop was the right thing to do."

"And where is this hiker?" Rob scanned the empty trailhead. "Why didn't we see them? Where did they park?"

"They changed their minds about the hike?" Travis backed out of the small parking area.

"Or maybe the person or persons who left the necklace there was the same person or persons who shot at Paige," Rob said. "They left the necklace because they wanted us to know they were watching. That they could, in fact, have taken us out if they had been so inclined."

"Could be," Travis said.

They drove to the sheriff's office, where Deputy Dwight Prentice greeted them at the door. "Hello, Rob," Dwight said. "Are you here because of the report on Henry Hake?"

"What report is that?" Rob asked.

"It must have come in while we were gone," Travis said. "Because I haven't heard about it, either." He led the way into his office and settled behind his desk. "Tell us about this report."

"The medical examiner's office sent over an up-dated report on their findings in Henry Hake's death," Dwight said. He handed a printout to Travis, who scanned it, his face giving away nothing. He passed the papers to Rob.

"I thought the ME ruled Henry Hake probably died of a heart attack," Rob said.

"He did," Dwight said. "But one of his bright young assistants got curious about some nasty-looking lesions on the body and did some more digging. This report is what he came up with."

Rob read quickly through it, only half listening as Dwight continued talking. His gaze shifted to the bottom section and the words *Conclusion: Death from Tularemia.*

"What is tularemia?" he asked.

"It's also called rabbit fever," Dwight said. "It's a naturally occurring bacteria that, if treated with antibiotics, is rarely fatal."

"And if untreated?" Travis asked.

"According to the Centers for Disease Control fact sheet attached to that report, a bite from an infected animal could cause skin ulcers, while inhaling the bacteria can lead to pneumonia or, in the most severe cases, typhoid-like symptoms," Dwight said.

"And the ME thinks that's what killed Henry Hake?" Travis looked skeptical. "Was he bitten by a rabbit or what?"

"Tularemia is one of the biological weapons the government experimented with in World War II," Dwight said. "It's one they were supposedly working on here in Rayford County. I remember reading about it." Recently, news about just such a secret government lab, located somewhere in the county, had come to light, causing a bit of a stir among history buffs.

Rob let out a low whistle.

"That government lab was supposedly located in an old mine somewhere near here," Travis said. "Could Henry Hake have picked it up in the soil while messing around looking for the lab?"

"Maybe," Dwight said. "But when I found his body, it was hanging from the ceiling in that underground chamber on the resort property—Hake didn't do that himself."

"You found the body after the DEA determined that chamber didn't have anything to do with either the World War II experiments or any modern crime," Rob said. "And the ME ruled Hake died weeks ago—so someone brought his body to that location after we left, and several weeks after he died."

"Right," Dwight said. "So while it's possible Hake died in that underground chamber and someone hid his body for a while, then brought it back, I don't think it's likely. Why go to all that trouble?"

"How would the government have used tularemia as a weapon?" Travis asked.

"Apparently, the idea was to put the bacteria in an aerosol," Dwight said. "You could put it in the ventilation system of a building or simply spray it over a crowd. Not everyone would catch the disease, and of those that did, not everyone would die."

"You said antibiotics will kill it," Rob said. "So it doesn't sound like a very practical weapon today."

"Except that most people wouldn't realize they had been exposed, or that they were suffering from tularemia," Dwight said. "Anyone with a compromised immune system, or lung or heart disease, might die before anyone figured out what was wrong."

"Henry Hake had a bad heart," Travis said.

"Did whoever killed him know that?" Rob asked.

"More unanswered questions," Travis said. "Would this be enough for the DEA to go back into that underground bunker and do some testing?"

"Maybe." Rob sighed. "I'm not even supposed to be here, you know."

"Your aunt wanted to know what really happened to Hake," Travis said. "This might be your best chance to find out."

Rob glanced at the clock on the wall by the door. "It's after five in DC, where the decision would have to be made," he said. "I'll contact my boss in the morning and let him take it from there." That would give him a few more hours to come up with a better explanation for why he was in Rayford County right now. Maybe he could persuade his boss he had just come here to fly-fish.

"Let us know what he says." Travis glanced at the report once more. "I wonder what the market is for biological weapons."

"What made you think of that?" Dwight asked.

"Because so many times these things come down to money," Travis said.

"My guess is there are terrorist groups who would hand over a lot of cash to get their hands on a weapon that was easy to distribute, tough to detect and effective for mass destruction," Rob said.

"Is there a weapon like that?" Dwight asked. "Tularemia doesn't sound like it would be very effective."

"Then maybe the point of the lab is to develop something better," Travis said. "It's one angle."

"Hake had a lot of money tied up in that resort project," Dwight said. "CNG Development talks like they want to spend even more money up there."

"Yet we've had two murders there—three, if you count Hake," Travis said. "As well as two accidental deaths, three people kidnapped, and a number of unexplained discharges of firearms up there."

"Maybe we can get the county to declare the place a public nuisance," Dwight said.

"More likely, CNG will complain that local law enforcement isn't doing a good job of keeping the criminal element off their property," Travis said. He straightened. "I'll give CNG a call and see what they have to say about this latest discovery."

"Let me know what they say," Rob said.

"Don't worry," Travis said. "You're part of this now, whether you want to be or not."

PAIGE TOLD HERSELF she had to trust Parker, as she watched him drive away. He was a good kid. Or rather, a good man. She had to remind herself her little brother wasn't a child anymore, and she shouldn't treat him like one. Yes, he had made some mistakes, but he was too smart to make those mistakes again. She wanted to believe this.

She checked the clock as she passed through the kitchen on the way to her office. It was after three thirty. She had expected her new guest, Robert Allen, to check in before now. Then again, maybe he had gotten a late start from Denver, or decided to do other things before showing up at the B and B. She asked that guests notify her only if they planned to arrive after 9:00 p.m.

She switched on her computer and prepared to focus on balancing her books and updating her financial records—a task guaranteed to require all her attention. She was deep into the frustration of trying to make her numbers agree with the bank's when the doorbell rang. She started and glanced at the clock, surprised to see she had been working for almost an hour. She closed her laptop and hurried to the door, fixing a smile in place, prepared to play the gracious hostess.

A check of the security peephole wiped the smile from her face. She unlocked the door and swept it open. "What do you think you're doing, following me around like this?" she demanded of a startled Rob Allerton.

He settled his features into his usual inscrutable expression. "I have a reservation," he said. "What are you doing here?"

"I own this place."

He glanced up at the neat white Victorian home,

with its black shutters, and neatly mulched flower beds filled with lilacs and peonies fading into winter dormancy. "Nice," he said.

"You're Robert Allen?" she asked.

He had the grace to wince. "The assistant who made the reservation must have automatically used my cover name," he said. "Sorry about that."

He made a move to walk past her into the house, but she stepped forward to join him on the front porch and shut the door behind her. "You can't stay here," she said.

"Why not?"

"Parker lives here now."

"I'm not interested in your brother," he said.

"I don't want to upset him." Parker had enough to deal with without having to face over the breakfast table every morning the man who had arrested him.

"We're all adults here," Rob said. "I don't see why there should be a problem."

"It's a problem for me. You'll have to find somewhere else to stay."

"Eagle Mountain doesn't have that many choices for accommodations," he said. "I spent plenty of time at the only motel while I was part of DEA's investigation into that underground lab."

"The motel is very nice," she said.

"It's adequate, but everyone there knows I'm a DEA agent. I prefer to keep this visit separate from that investigation. This is a personal visit and I'd like to keep to the appearance of a relaxing vacation as much as possible. When my assistant suggested a B and B I liked the idea."

Paige crossed her arms and scowled at him. She had the right to refuse service to anyone, but he could make a big stink if he wanted to. And turning away a paying customer at this slow time of year would be foolish, wouldn't it? But to have this man, who had almost ruined Parker's life, in her home—well, Rob had helped to almost ruin Parker's life, since she couldn't deny that Parker was the one who was mostly to blame. Still, it galled her to think of having Rob living here for the next week.

"What are you afraid of?" Rob asked. "If you're that worried, you can lock your door. Or should I lock mine?"

She wanted to slap the wolfish smile off his face, but before she could raise her hand, he grabbed her by the shoulders and shoved her to the ground. For the second time that day she found herself fighting him as he held her down. Then gunfire exploded very near her ear and tore into the door where she had been standing only seconds before.

Chapter Five

Paige's scream merged with the screech of tires and the roar of an engine as the black sedan raced down the street in front of the Bear's Den B and B. Rob, his weapon drawn, straightened and peered at the retreating car. There was no license plate, and the darkly tinted windows prevented him from seeing the occupants. Though there had been at least two people inside—the driver and the person who had fired the gun out the passenger window.

"What happened?" Paige asked, her voice shaky. She tried to sit up and this time he let her. He returned the gun to the holster at his hip, then reached down and pulled her to her feet.

"Was someone shooting at us?" she asked.

"Yes." He turned his attention from the street to look at her more closely. "Are you all right?" he asked.

"I'm okay." She rubbed her elbow. "Just a little banged up."

"Sorry if I was a little rough," he said. "I glimpsed the gun and had to move fast." He had acted on pure instinct, pushing her out of danger, shielding her with his own body.

"I'm okay," she said again. She straightened her blouse. "Who was it? Was it the men from the resort property? The ones who shot at me before?"

Rob shook his head. "I don't know. I didn't get a good look at them. I saw their silhouettes and the gun." He pulled his phone from his pocket and dialed the sheriff's office—Travis's direct number.

Travis answered on the second ring. "Hello?"

"This is Rob Allerton. I'm at Paige Riddell's place. A black sedan, tinted windows, no plates, two men inside, just drove by and fired on us."

"Dwight is already on his way over," Travis said. "We had a report of gunfire in the area. Is anyone hurt?"

"No. Some damage to the front door." He surveyed the line of bullet holes across the bright red door, like a row of stitches. His roller bag sat inches from the door, but was unscathed.

"I think I need to sit down." Paige sank onto the bench beside the door, her head between her knees. Rob walked out to the street and studied the angle of the shot. He had parked his truck in the paved area between the B and B and the house to the left—which meant anyone driving by had a clear view of the front porch where he and Paige had been standing. The house was only about a hundred feet from the street, making for an easy target.

As he stood at the curb, a Rayford County Sheriff's Department SUV pulled up. Dwight rolled down the passenger window and leaned toward Rob. "I just heard from Travis. You and Paige okay?"

He glanced over his shoulder to where Paige sat, upright now, hands gripping the edge of the bench, staring at the floor between her feet. "She's a little shaken up," he said. "But she'll be okay."

"We've got a BOLO on the car you described," Dwight said. "Can you show me where the bullets hit?"

The two men walked up on the porch. "Hello, Paige," Dwight said. "You okay?"

She nodded.

"Did you get a look at the shooter?" Dwight asked.

"I never saw them. Rob pushed me out of the way before I even knew they were there."

Dwight nodded, then bent to examine the damaged door. He took some photos. "At least some of the bullets are embedded in the door," he said. "We'll get someone out here to collect them. Is there anything else you can tell me—about the car or the shooters?"

"I'm sorry," Paige said. "I can't think of anything."

"We'll do our best to patrol here more frequently," Dwight said. "But you might want to think about staying somewhere else for a while."

She stared at him. "I can't do that. I have guests. And Parker is here."

Dwight's eyes met Rob's. "It would be better if you went somewhere safer," Dwight repeated.

"How do you know I was even the target?" Paige

asked, with more strength in her voice. "I imagine a DEA agent has made all kinds of enemies."

Rob looked at the door again. "Maybe so," he said. "But the shots were fired where you were standing."

Her face paled, but she set her jaw. "I'm not leaving my home and my business," she said.

"I can't force you," Dwight said.

"I'm staying here," Rob said. "I'll keep an eye on things."

"Let us know if you see anything suspicious." Dwight nodded to Paige, then left.

When they were alone again, Rob turned to Paige. "Where's Parker?" he asked.

"He's out."

"Out where?"

"None of your business."

He almost smiled. This was the Paige he was used to. "Do you know where he is?" he asked.

"He's an adult. I don't keep track of his every move."

Somehow he doubted this was a philosophy she had adopted willingly, having seen her mother-bear act in court. "Do you want me to call him?" he asked.

"No!"

"I thought maybe you would feel better with him here."

"No. There's no need to worry him."

"Did you tell him about what happened this morning? The other shooting?"

"No. He doesn't need to know."

"There's such a thing as being too independent, you know," Rob said.

She stood. "Come on. Let's get you checked in."

He could have pressed the issue, but what would be the point? Paige wasn't going to change on his say-so. He reclaimed his roller bag from beside the door and followed her inside.

The interior of the home was comfortably furnished with a mixture of antique and contemporary pieces. Art on the walls depicted local scenery. Rob saw none of the chintz and cutesiness he had feared when his admin had suggested a B and B for his stay. Instead, the decor was low-key and classy— like Paige herself.

She moved to a small desk in what must have been the home's front parlor or formal living room and unlocked an adjacent cabinet to reveal a computer. "What name is on the credit card you'll be using?" she asked, typing.

"Robert Allerton."

"Not Robert Allen?"

"As I said before, I'm not here on business." Not exactly. He had sworn his admin to secrecy. After he talked to his boss in the morning, he might be assigned to the case, but for now, he was on his own dime.

She scanned the card he handed her, then returned it, along with a set of old-fashioned keys on a brass fob. "The round one is for the front door," she said. "The other is for your room. You're in the Grizzly Suite. Turn left at the top of the stairs and go all the way to the end of the hallway. Breakfast is from seven to nine each morning."

He replaced the card in his wallet. "Dwight was right," he said. "You'd be safer if you moved to a location that was unknown to whoever is targeting you."

"I have a business to run and a life to live. I can't stop everything to go hide out in a cave somewhere until you or Dwight or whoever decides it's safe to come out. I'll be smart and take precautions, but I won't do what these men want."

"What do you think they want?" he asked.

She shut the cabinet door and locked it. "For me to keep quiet about what I saw. That has to be the reason they want me dead. They think they can frighten me into shutting up. But all they've done is make me more determined to find out what is going on up there."

She started to move from behind the desk, but Rob blocked her, one hand on her arm, near enough that when she inhaled sharply, the tips of her breasts brushed his sleeve. He fought the urge to pull her close and kiss the protest from her lips. Did she have any idea how maddening and enticing he found her? "Don't get any ideas about investigating this on your own," he said. "That could be dangerous."

"I'll be careful."

Careful might not be enough, but he wasn't going to get anywhere arguing with her about it. He moved aside and started to turn toward the stairs, but she put out a hand to stop him, then grabbed hold of the sleeve of his jacket. "Rob?"

He turned back, looking into her eyes, which were the color of storm clouds, fringed with thick brown lashes. Eyes that could make a man forget every angry word she had ever leveled at him. "Yes?"

She swallowed, color rising in her cheeks. "Thank you."

"What are you thanking me for?"

"For saving my life."

He could have dismissed this with a denial that he had done anything special. He had reacted on pure instinct, with no time to think about what he was doing or why. But he wouldn't let her off the hook that easily. "You know that old superstition," he said.

Two shallow lines formed between her eyebrows. "What old superstition?"

"When you save a person's life, then you're responsible for them."

She released her hold on him as if she had been scorched. "No man is responsible for me."

He smiled, a heated curve of his lips that had reduced more than one woman to breathlessness. "Have I ever told you I'm a very superstitious person? And I take my responsibilities very seriously." He leaned forward and kissed her cheek, feeling the heat of her skin and breathing in the herbal scent of her shampoo.

When he stepped back, he half expected her to slap him. Maybe he even deserved it, but that kiss had been worth it. Instead, she only tried to wound him with her gaze. Still smiling, he picked up his bag and headed for the stairs, taking them two at a time to the second floor. His stay at the Bear's Den was going to be very interesting, indeed.

Chapter Six

Paige lay awake for hours that night, reliving every moment of being shot at—the sound of the bullets, the fear that had threatened to choke her, the feel of Rob's weight on her, crushing and frightening and yet so reassuring. The man was maddening, one moment so tender and protective, the next knowing exactly what to say to make her angry. All that non-sense about him being responsible for her—and then he'd had the nerve to kiss her.

That the kiss hadn't been on the lips unnerved her even more. If he had insisted on kissing her mouth, she could have told herself he had practically as-saulted her, and that he'd taken liberties to which he wasn't entitled. But that gentle brush of his lips against her cheek had been both tender and incred-ibly sensuous. She still trembled at the memory, at the intensity of her awareness of him—the scent of his aftershave, the soft cotton of his shirtsleeve, the incredible heat of his mouth.

She shouldn't have let him get away with it. She should have told him off then and there. But she couldn't find the words to do it. When he had left her, still smiling that *I'm-so-sexy* grin, she had had to bite her lip to keep from calling him back. In that moment, if he had tried to kiss her mouth, she would have pulled him to her willingly.

After that, it took a long time for her to drift into a restless sleep. She woke several hours later with a start and stared into the darkness, heart pounding. She held her breath and strained her ears to listen. Yes, that was definitely the sound of the back door opening. She turned her head to check the bedside clock. One thirty-two. She heard shuffling, then the sound of someone walking—no, tiptoeing—past her door.

She sat up and switched on the lamp. "Parker, is that you?" she called.

"Yes. Go back to sleep."

Instead, she got up and went to the bedroom door and opened it. Parker stood in the hallway, hair rumpled, shoulders slumped. Her first instinct was to demand to know where he had been, but she stifled the words. "You look tired," she said instead.

He shrugged. "I'm okay." He turned away. "Good night."

"Wait," she said. "There's something I need to tell you."

He stopped, but didn't look back at her. "What is it?"

"Rob Allerton is here," she said.

"Yeah. You already told me he's in town. So what?"

"No—he's here."

He did turn this time, and craned his neck, trying to see past her into her room. "Here?"

She flushed, even though the suggestion that Agent Rob Allerton would be in her bed was preposterous. "He's upstairs. In the Grizzly Suite. He has a reservation for a week."

"Okay."

She leaned forward, studying her brother more closely. He needed a shave, and he had the beginnings of dark circles under his eyes. Was he really just tired, or was something more going on? She pushed the thought away. She had to trust him. "You're okay with him being here?"

"I guess his money is as good as anybody else's. And it's not like I'll see him much, between work and school and stuff."

Stuff. What stuff? But she didn't ask. "It's probably a good idea if you stay out of his way as much as possible," she said.

"Don't worry. I will."

"He didn't make a reservation here because of you," she said. "He didn't even know I owned the place."

"Right." He smirked.

"He didn't," she protested.

"You can believe that if you want. I think Agent Allerton knew exactly what he was doing."

She resented everything his words—and that smirk—implied. "I actually asked him to leave, but there's another reason he needs to be here right now."

Parker leaned one shoulder against the wall, arms folded across his chest. "I'm really tired, sis. Can we make this quick?"

She wet her lips. He was probably going to find out sooner or later. Better she tell him rather than have him hear the gossip from someone else. "Someone took a shot at me while I was hiking up by Eagle Mountain Resort yesterday," she said.

He straightened. "What?"

"I saw two men on the resort property. One of them spotted me watching them and tried to shoot me. Later, a car—possibly with the same two men inside—drove by here and someone shot at me again. Rob pushed me out of the way. As it is, the front door is ruined and will have to be replaced."

"Sis! What have you done?"

"What have I done? I haven't done anything."

"You must have done something to tick off these guys enough to try to take you out."

"I didn't do anything," she said again. "But until the authorities can track down those men, I thought it wouldn't be a bad idea for Rob to stay here. He does have some experience with situations like this."

"You mean he's got a gun and he knows how to use it." Parker shook his head, as if trying to clear it, then looked at her more closely. "Are you sure you're okay?"

"I'm fine." A little shaky still, but she was determined to get past that. And her little brother's concern touched her. "I really think Rob scared them away yesterday," she said. "And now the sheriff's department and probably other law enforcement agencies are looking for them. I don't think they'll bother me again."

"I hope not." He ran one hand through his hair. "You say you were up by Eagle Mountain Resort the first time? This morning?"

"Yes. I was on the hiking trail that runs alongside the resort. You remember—we went up there right after you moved to town."

He nodded. "Why didn't you tell me about it this morning?"

"I didn't want to worry you. And I certainly didn't think they would track me down here."

"It's not hard to find anybody in a town this small," Parker said. "Maybe you should go away for a while, until this is all over."

"No!" The word came out louder than she intended. She lowered her voice. "I'll be careful, but I won't put my whole life on hold and hide."

"What were those guys doing up at the resort?" Parker asked.

"I don't know," she said. "I saw them carrying a big wooden box into a hole in the ground."

"That underground chamber where Gage and his girlfriend were trapped a couple months ago?" Parker asked.

"Maybe. I don't know. I'm going to try to find out."

"Don't go up there again," Parker said.

"If I do go, I won't go alone," she said.

"Get Rob to go with you. Or better yet, stay home."

"I don't want Rob to go with me. Maybe Gage can come."

"Rob wants to be your bodyguard, why not let him?" Parker yawned.

"Go to bed," Paige said. "And don't worry about me."

"I figure I probably owe you a little worrying." He patted her shoulder, then turned and shuffled down the hall to his room. Paige returned to her room and bed, but didn't go to sleep. She was going to end up back at the resort sooner or later, she knew. She wouldn't go alone, but she wouldn't sit here doing nothing and waiting for others to solve this mystery.

MAYA RENFRO WAS a petite dynamo whose shoulder-length black hair was streaked with blue. Even at seven thirty in the morning, she bounced into the Cake Walk Café with all the energy she displayed as coach of Eagle Mountain High's girls' basketball team. "Paige, it's so good to see you," she said. "And wow, doesn't this place look great? I haven't been here since they reopened. Gage told me a driver crashed into it this summer."

"Yes. The owner, Iris Desmet, decided as long as she was rebuilding, she would expand and add a coffee bar." She ushered her friend to a table. "How are you? And how is Casey?" Casey was Maya's five-year-old niece, who lived with Maya and Gage since her parents' murders that summer.

"She's great. Last week she asked if, when Gage and I get married, she can change her name, too, so we all match." Maya snatched a paper napkin from the dispenser on the table and dabbed at her eyes. "Sorry—I still get teary thinking about it."

"That's terrific," Paige said. "I guess she's really taken to Gage?"

"He's amazing," Maya said. "For a man who swore he was a confirmed bachelor, he's turning out to be a really great father. We don't want Casey to ever forget her real parents, but it's nice to think the three of us can be a new family together."

She pulled out a chair and sank into it. "Now you've heard all about me—what did you want to see me about so early in the morning?"

"I wanted to catch you before school." And before Rob was up, watching her and questioning her. Paige sat across from Maya. "I hate to bring up a painful subject, but I wanted to ask about the underground chamber up at Eagle Mountain Resort where you and Gage and Casey were held prisoner."

Maya's smile vanished and her shoulders slumped. "What about it?"

"Where was it on the property, exactly?"

"Paige, why would you want to know that?"

She shifted in her chair. "It's kind of a long story."

"Buy me a latte and I'll give you all the time you need."

Two vanilla soy lattes later, Paige had spilled the whole story of seeing the two men disappear into a trapdoor in the forest floor with a mysterious crate, how they had later shot at her, and the drive-by shooting at her home.

"Wow!" Maya said, when the story concluded. "It definitely sounds like you stumbled onto something big. But I don't think the trapdoor you saw was over the chamber where Gage and I were."

"No?"

"No." Maya sipped her latte, then wiped foam from above her lips. "We weren't near the fence at all. I'm surprised Travis didn't tell you that already."

"I wanted to double-check." After all, Maya was the one who had been held prisoner in that chamber.

"What I don't get is why bother going through a trapdoor when there was an exit right onto the resort's main street?" Maya asked.

"So, maybe there's another chamber?" Paige said.

"Maybe there are a bunch of them. There are a lot of mines in the mountains around here, and mine tunnels, right?"

"I guess so."

"Have you talked to Gage about any of this?" Maya asked.

"No. I thought it would be easier to talk to you. I mean, he can't really tell me anything because he's a cop."

"I might be a little prejudiced, but I think he's a good one," Maya said. "You should leave the investigating to him."

"I'm not investigating," Paige said. "I'm just curious. After all, those bullets were aimed at me. You can't blame me for wanting to know why. I wonder if

I can get my hands on a map of the resort. Maybe the planning commission has something." She frowned. "Of course, they won't let me look at it."

"Why not?"

"The mayor, Larry Rowe, was head of the planning commission before he ran for mayor. He still has a grudge against me because my environmental group kept the project from going forward."

"You need to be careful," Maya said. "A lot of bad things have happened that are associated with the resort property. You couldn't pay me to go up there again."

"I understand why you feel that way," Paige said. "But if everyone avoids the property, it allows whoever is up there to get away with whatever they want. Whatever they were hiding in that space was something they didn't want me to see. I want to find out what it was and expose them."

"You need to let the sheriff's department do that."

"I will let them handle anything that turns out to be illegal," Paige said. "But that doesn't mean that, as an ordinary citizen, I can't ask questions and try to gather information. It's what I'm trained to do, as an activist."

"So who are you going to question about all of this?" Maya asked.

"I'll start with the new owners of the property, CNG Development."

"I'm sure Travis and Gage have already thought of that."

"I'm sure they have," Paige said. "But these corporate types won't tell the cops anything. They'll talk to me. How do you think I got the scoop on Eagle Mountain Resort? I made phone calls and asked questions. There's nothing dangerous about that."

"It sounds safe enough." Maya pushed aside her empty cup. "As long as you don't ask the wrong person the wrong question."

"I'll be careful." Truth be told, she was excited about the prospect. Since they'd won the injunction against building Eagle Mountain Resort and the challenge over the gate blocking the Dakota Ridge Trail, life had felt a little stale. She looked forward to the challenge of finding out what was really happening on the former resort property. She would succeed where others had failed.

DEA SENIOR DETECTIVE Dale Foster was a busy man with no patience for time wasting, so when Rob placed his call to his supervisor the next morning, he got right to the point. "I'm here in Eagle Mountain," he said. "Sheriff Walker has requested the DEA re-open our investigation of that underground laboratory we looked into up here last month."

"What are you doing in Eagle Mountain?" Foster asked. "And why did the sheriff contact you instead of contacting our office?"

"I came to do some fly-fishing," Rob lied. "I ran into the sheriff yesterday and he relayed the request."

"Humph."

Rob's gut clenched. So much for thinking he would get away with that lame explanation.

"Why does Walker want us to reopen the investigation?" Foster asked. "You told me you didn't find anything. I trust you went over the location thoroughly."

"I did. But we were looking for any indication of illegal drug manufacturing. The sheriff suspects something else might have been going on down there."

"What?" Foster barked the word, an impatient man becoming more impatient.

"The week after we left, one of Walker's deputies found a dead man in the location," Rob said. "He had been missing about a month, and the medical examiner confirms he had been dead about that long, but someone had strung up his body in that old lab space underground. Originally, the ME was unable to determine the cause of death, but more recent tests indicate the man died from exposure to tularemia."

"What is tularemia?"

"Rabbit fever. But of more interest to us, it's something that the US government considered as a possible biological weapon in World War II. You remember in my report I mentioned that we were asked to rule out the lab's use during that time period."

"And you determined nothing in the lab was that old. So I repeat—what does this have to do with us?"

"Walker wants us to take another look, see if we can detect any tularemia in the space."

"Tell him to call the health department. That's not under our purview."

Rob had expected this answer. Like every government agency these days, the DEA was chronically underfunded and understaffed. "I'll tell him, sir."

"When are you coming back to work?" Foster asked.

"I have six days left on my vacation," Rob said.

"Humph." This time the sound was uttered with a little less ire behind it.

"Is there anything else you'd like me to tell Sheriff Walker?" Rob asked.

"Tell him I'm sorry we can't help him. And, Allerton?"

"Yes, sir?"

"Let the sheriff handle this. You stick to fish."

"Of course, sir."

They ended the conversation and Rob tucked his phone back into the pocket of his jeans. The only fish he wanted to catch right now were the two men who had fired those shots yesterday. If they led him to the real reason for Henry Hake's death, so much the better. But he'd be careful not to act in any official capacity.

He stepped out of the room, locking the door behind him. When he turned he was surprised to see Parker Riddell walking toward him. The young man looked healthier than he had the last time Rob had seen him—he had gained a few pounds and lost the sickly pallor Rob associated with addicts. "Hello, Parker," he said.

"Hey." He stopped in front of Rob, arms crossed over his chest, expression somber. "Paige told me what happened," he said. "With those guys shooting at her, up at the resort, and here in front of the house."

"I tried to persuade her to leave until this was resolved," Rob said. "She refused."

"Yeah, well, no surprise there. Look up *stubborn* in the dictionary and there's Paige's picture." He ran a hand through his close-cropped hair. "I need to ask you a favor."

"Oh?" Rob waited, wary. It wasn't as if he and this young man were on friendly terms.

"Look after her," Parker said. "I mean, I can't be here all the time, but she said you're on vacation, and you're here anyway, so maybe it wouldn't be a real hardship on you to stay close."

"Paige doesn't like me."

Parker didn't exactly smile, but his expression did lighten. "Oh, she likes you. She just doesn't want to admit it. Since that fiasco with her ex she likes to pretend she doesn't need a man in her life, but it's all bluff."

"What was the fiasco with her ex?" This was the first Rob had heard about an ex.

Parker frowned. "I don't know the whole story, but I guess he started out nice when they first married and ended up being a real jerk. I don't know if he actually hit her, or just threatened her, but they sure didn't end up on speaking terms, and ever since she's been kind of standoffish with men."

Rob supposed he could take comfort in knowing he wasn't being singled out for the cold shoulder. But the idea that a man—Paige's husband—had threatened her made him feel like finding the guy and making him regret he had ever come near her.

"I'm sorry to hear that," Rob said, his voice deceptively mild.

"Honestly, I think one of the reasons she's so hostile toward you—besides the trouble you and I had—is that she's attracted to you and fighting it," Parker said.

Was Paige attracted to him, or was Parker pouring it on thick to get him to stick around? "I'll keep an eye on her," he said. "As much as she'll let me."

"Thanks." Paige's brother shoved his hands in his pockets, apparently not ready to leave.

"Is there something else?" Rob asked.

Parker sighed. "Yeah. Last night, she talked about going back up to the resort and trying to find out what's going on. Don't let her go alone. I mean, I get that she wants to be independent, but she's not bulletproof."

"I won't let her go up there—alone or otherwise."

"Good. Well, I need to go. I have a class." He nodded and shuffled off.

Downstairs, the dining room off the kitchen was empty. A long cherry table held a single place setting, with a linen napkin, gold-trimmed china plate and polished flatware. A fruit cup in a crystal dish sat in the center of the plate, and a buffet against the wall held a silver coffee service and two covered chafing dishes.

As Rob stood surveying the scene, Paige came

in from the kitchen carrying a bakery box. "Good morning," she said.

"This looks impressive," he said, indicating the table. "Am I your only guest?"

"I have an older couple staying a few nights. They were up early and are already off for a day of Jeeping on the backcountry trails." She began arranging muffins on a glass serving tray. "There's an egg casserole in the chafing dish," she said. "Help yourself."

He moved the fruit cup to one side, carried the plate to the buffet and selected a muffin from the tray. "You're up and about early."

"I like to get an early start."

"Do you have time to have coffee with me?" he asked, before she could retreat to the kitchen.

She hesitated, then sat in the chair across from him. "What are your plans for the day?" she asked, as he sat and tucked into his breakfast.

"That depends." He sipped the coffee, which was hot and strong, exactly the way he preferred it. "What are *your* plans?"

"Why are you asking?"

"Because I'm staying with you." He split the muffin—blueberry—and slid in a pat of butter.

"Rob, I—"

"Don't argue, Paige." He bit into the muffin and had to suppress a sigh. It practically melted in his mouth. He swallowed and picked up his fork. "Did you make all this? It's delicious."

"I picked them up at the Cake Walk Café earlier

this morning," she said. "And don't change the subject. I don't need you to babysit me."

"We both know you'll be safer with someone to watch your back. You do what you need to do and try to forget I'm here." He savored the first bite of the egg-cheese-and-sausage casserole.

She snorted—an unladylike and at the same time endearing sound. Or maybe he was being influenced by the amazing breakfast.

She sipped her coffee, then set the cup down with a clink against the saucer. "I need to see about getting the door replaced, order some supplies and run some errands," she said.

"Consider me your chauffeur."

"I don't need—"

He set down his fork and looked her in the eye. "Maybe you don't, but I do. I need to know you're safe."

Her lips parted and her eyes widened. If the table hadn't been between them, he would have been tempted to lean across and kiss her, just to see what kind of reaction he would get. Had Parker been right when he had said she was attracted to him? Was the attraction strong enough for her to act on it?

"Why do you care?" she asked. "And don't give me that line about being responsible for me now."

He sat back, hiding his disappointment. No, she wasn't *that* attracted to him. "How about this for a reason?" he asked. "You may be our best chance of solving this case."

"How do you figure that?"

"We want to catch these guys and find out what they're up to. You're the only one who got a good look at them. They want you. If they do try to come after you again, we want to be ready."

"So you want to use me as bait?" Her voice rose on the last word, almost a squeak.

"No. I'm not going to let you wait for them out in the open. But if they do come back, I'm going to be here and I'm going to be ready to stop them."

She nodded, subdued. "All right."

She remained silent while he finished his breakfast, his attention focused on the food, though he was acutely aware of the woman across from him, close enough to brush his hand against. But she might as well have worn a sign around her neck that declared Don't Touch.

The doorbell rang and she jumped. "Are you expecting someone?" he asked.

"No." She stared toward the door, but didn't move. Deny it all she liked, she was clearly still upset by what had happened yesterday.

He pushed back his chair, wiped his mouth and dropped the napkin on his empty plate. "Let's go see who it is."

Chapter Seven

Rob had probably intended to lead the way to the front door, but Paige stepped in front of him. After all, this was her house. Whoever was there wanted to see her. She wasn't going to let what had happened yesterday keep her from answering her own door. He trailed behind her. The doorbell sounded again and her stomach fluttered as if she had swallowed live eels. She shoved her nervousness aside and focused instead on how angry it made her that two lowlifes she didn't even know had frightened her this way.

Relief flooded her when she looked through the security peephole and saw the calm face of the sheriff looking back at her. She unlocked the door and swung it open. "Have you found something?" she asked.

"We haven't found the men who shot at you," he said. He looked down at the splintered door. "Only the one burst of fire? They didn't try a second round of shots?"

"I already had Paige on the ground and returned fire." Rob stepped forward, one hand on Paige's shoulder. She should have resisted the gesture, but instead, she had to fight not to lean back into his strength. "They probably didn't want to risk sticking around," Rob said.

"I'm having the door replaced today," Paige said. "As soon as I file a claim with my insurance company."

"Adelaide can give you a case number if they need it," Travis said. "May I come in?"

"Of course." She stepped back and he moved past her. Rob shut and locked the door.

"Let's go in here," Travis said, leading the way into the dining room. He took an envelope from his pocket and emptied its contents onto the table.

"My necklace," she said, and scooped up the gold chain with the familiar bird charm.

"Is this the necklace you lost up by the resort?" Travis asked.

"Yes. Where did you find it?"

"Rob and I went up to the trail yesterday after we talked to you and took a look around," Travis said. "When we got back to my SUV, someone had taped this to the driver's-side door."

"They made sure we didn't miss it," Rob said.

"Another hiker must have found it and assumed it belonged to whoever was in your vehicle," she said. She examined the necklace. It was unharmed. "Or maybe they just wanted to turn it in to the police."

"We didn't see anyone else on the trail coming or going," Rob said. "We didn't pass any other cars or hear anyone, or see anyone on the other side of the fence at the resort. And there were no other cars in the parking area."

She looked from one man to the other. Their serious expressions were starting to worry her. "Someone must have been up there," she said. "Someone had to leave the necklace for you."

"We're thinking it was someone who didn't want us to see them," Rob said. "Someone who wanted us to know they knew about you."

A shudder went through her at the words. "Why would they do that?" She tried to put on the necklace, fumbling with the clasp.

Rob stepped up behind her. "Let me." His fingers brushed the back of her neck as he fastened the necklace, sending heat radiating through her.

"I don't know what their motives might have been," Travis said. "Maybe it is as simple as them wanting the necklace returned to you. It's possible the person who put the necklace there didn't have anything to do with the shooting. Have you remembered anything else about the men you saw yesterday that can help us find them?"

Rob had finished hooking the necklace, but he remained standing behind her, one hand on her shoulder. She told herself she should move away from him, but couldn't make herself do it. "I'm sorry—no," she said. "Everything happened so fast."

"I've got a call in to CNG Development," Travis said. "We want permission to go up there and search. I'm waiting to hear back from them."

"I talked to my boss this morning," Rob said. "He

says this really is out of our area of expertise. He suggested you contact the public health department. Maybe they can test for tularemia in that lab."

Travis nodded. "That's a good idea—if we can get permission to go back in."

Paige looked from one man to the other. "Tularemia? What the heck is that?"

"Rabbit fever," Rob said.

When he didn't offer anything more, she glared at him. "Why do you care about rabbit fever?"

"It's one of the agents the government was supposedly testing during World War II for use as a weapon," Travis said.

"And?" she asked.

"And I can't tell you anything else."

She frowned. It wasn't the answer she wanted, but about what she had expected. "Is there anything else you can tell me about this case? Any leads on the men who fired on me, or their vehicle?"

The sheriff shook his head. "We don't have anything yet, but we're going to keep looking." He turned to Rob. "Are you going to be around for a while?"

"I'm here all week, but not in an official capacity," Rob said.

"If I needed backup, could you help out?"

"Yes."

"Good. I'll keep it in mind."

"I want to go back up there," Paige said. "To the resort."

Both men looked at her as if she had sprouted an extra head. "That's a bad idea," Rob said.

"I agree," Travis said. "I'm considering closing the trail to public access until we get to the bottom of this."

"You can't close the trail unless you station someone at the trailhead to enforce the order," Paige said. "And you don't have the manpower to do that. Besides, it's not as if that many people go up there."

"You don't need to go up there," Travis said.

"I'll be fine," she said. "And I'll take my bodyguard." She looked at Rob.

"You can't go on CNG property without their permission," Travis said.

"I know. I'll stay on the public side of the fence. I just want—I need—to take another look at the scene. Maybe being there again will trigger my memory of something that will help you find these men."

Travis gave her a hard look, but she met his gaze and didn't flinch. "All right," he said. "Then I guess that means we're all going. Together."

TRAVIS HAD A meeting he had to attend, so they agreed to meet up at the sheriff's department later that afternoon. Paige had spent her morning with Rob by her side, dealing with her insurance company and arranging to have the front door replaced. He had been quiet and unobtrusive, but there was no ignoring his presence— filling up the room. What was it about the man that he seemed to take up so much space, and use up more than his share of oxygen?

"Don't you have something else you need to be doing?" she asked.

"Not really."

"You didn't take a week's vacation to hang out with me."

"I can think of worse ways to spend my time." He sat back in his chair, regarding her with a hint of a smile, eyelids at half-mast. His expression should have come across as lazy and indolent, but instead conveyed a feline sensuality, as if he was feigning his lack of energy and at any moment might pounce. "You're almost pleasant when you aren't angry with me."

"You're making me nervous," she said.

"Interesting. You don't strike me as a woman who is easily unnerved."

She shuffled the papers on the table in front of her. "I think having your life threatened twice in one day would upset anyone."

He sat up straight. His flirtatious mood had vanished. "You're right," he said. "I didn't mean to make light of what happened."

"I've been going over and over everything so much my head hurts." She pushed the papers—insurance forms and measurements for the new door—aside. "Let's talk about something else."

"Such as?"

"If we're going to be spending so much time together, we should get to know each other better. I really don't know much about you."

"All right," he said. "What would you like to know?"

"Have you ever been married?"

He blinked. He obviously hadn't been expecting

that one. Why did it feel like such a victory to throw Mr. Cool off guard? "No," he said.

"Why not?"

He shrugged. "I never found the right woman."

"What a cliché. You can do better than that, can't you?" She leaned across the table toward him. "Are you afraid of making a commitment?"

"You're one to talk, Ms. Independent." He scooted his chair closer. "Though I understand you've been married before. What was he like?"

"How did you know that?" Had he been checking up on her?

"Parker mentioned it."

"Parker? When?"

"This morning, actually. He came to my room and asked me to look after you."

A storm of emotions swept over her—tenderness, sadness, annoyance. "That really wasn't necessary," she said.

"Maybe not. It made me curious about your ex, though."

"My ex was not a nice person." She slid her chair back. "And that's all I'm going to say on the subject." Her marriage had been a bad time in her life, when a man she had made the mistake of trusting had used love as a weapon to break her. It had taken a long time for her to find her way back to herself after that. Like someone who had suffered a long, debilitating illness, she had had to build her strength slowly. She was determined to never again go back to that dark place.

Rob looked as if he wanted to argue, but he thought better of it. "Parker looked good," he said. "Healthy."

"He is. Good and healthy."

"He said he had a class this morning. What's he studying?"

"History. I told him there weren't many jobs in that field, but he's convinced he can make it work. And it's a subject he loves, so I'm not going to discourage him. Right now he's just taking the basics, with a couple of extra history courses thrown in. And he's working, as a delivery driver for Peggy's Pizza here in town. And he volunteers at the local history museum."

Rob nodded. "He's keeping busy. That's good."

"He is good. He's staying out of trouble."

"Has he made friends here in town? A girlfriend, maybe?"

Did Parker have a girlfriend? Why hadn't she wondered about that before? "I don't think so," she said. Though maybe that explained where he was disappearing to in his off hours. But if it was a girl, why hadn't he said so? Did he think she wouldn't approve?

Paige realized Rob had continued talking. "I'm sorry," she said. "I was thinking of something else. What did you say?"

"I asked if he planned to continue living here with you for a while."

"At least until he finishes school," she said. "Why shouldn't he? I like having him here."

"No reason," Rob said. "I just wondered. I wish him luck."

If he was so concerned about Parker's future, why had he been so dogged in sending him to jail? But that was an old argument that wasn't worth rehashing. "Why did you go into law enforcement?" she asked. "And why the DEA? Don't you get tired of arresting people and putting them in jail?"

His expression hardened. "The people I arrest need to be stopped and punished. Don't forget that I put away the people who make the drugs that ruin lives—the way Parker's life was almost ruined."

"All right. I'll concede that you probably do some good."

"So what is your problem?"

"Law enforcement sees the world in black-and-white. I see so many shades of gray."

"No, you don't," he countered. "You see the world in black-and-white, too, but your definition of black-and-white is different from mine, so that makes me wrong."

"That's not true!"

"I don't want to argue with you." He leaned toward her. "We can admit that the two of us are never going to agree on everything, but we don't have to be adversaries. People like me can sharpen your vision—and people like you can temper mine."

Where was the hard-nosed officer she had sparred with when Parker was awaiting trial and sentencing? It embarrassed her a little to remember some of the shouting matches they had had in the courthouse hallways back then. The man across from her now was smart and reasonable—and even compassionate. "I never thought of it that way before," she said. "But I guess you're right."

He sat back. "And I know how much you hate to admit that."

"I guess you're doing it already," she said. "Trying to sharpen my vision."

"And what do you see?"

She saw a man who was more nuanced than she had given him credit for. A man who tempted her to be far more vulnerable than she liked. Rob made her think about taking risks—an exhilarating feeling, but one she wasn't sure she would have the courage to act on. She stood. "Come on. It's almost time to meet Travis," she said.

She walked out of the room, aware of his gaze on her as she moved past him. It had all the force and heat of a physical caress.

ROB AND PAIGE met Travis and Gage at the sheriff's department and caravanned to the parking area for the Dakota Ridge Trail. "We can't trespass on CNG property," Travis said. "The company has referred me to their lawyers, but the legal team hasn't returned my calls."

"I checked this morning and the gate is still locked and there's no sign of anyone around the place," Gage said. "Of course, we have the authority to break the lock."

"Which I don't want to do if we don't have to,"

Travis said. "If no one is around, there's no point.
Without a warrant, we can't search any of the buildings."

"So what's the plan?" Rob asked.

"Paige thinks retracing her steps that day might help
her remember more about what happened," Travis said.
"So that's what we'll do." He motioned for her to lead
the way.

She shouldered the day pack she had brought and
started up the trail, Rob close behind her. She walked
quickly, with a sure stride, her head up, back straight.
If she was nervous, she certainly didn't show it.

No one said anything for the first quarter mile of
walking, until the trail began to parallel the former
resort property's fence. Paige slowed, scanning the
fence line, until she came to the break in the underbrush that Travis and Rob had investigated the day
before. "I think about here was where I heard something and ducked to the side to look." She parted the
low-growing branches of scrub oak with her hands
and darted into the open space next to the fence. Rob
and Travis followed, crowding in close around her.
Gage stayed on the trail to keep watch.

For the second time in as many days, Rob looked
through the fence to a stretch of vacant forest, at dry
leaves carpeting the ground beneath the white trunks
of aspens and the dark green branches of evergreens.
Nothing disturbed the peacefulness of the scene, and

the only sound was the soft whisper of the dry aspen leaves that still clung to the trees.

"What's that?" Travis whispered. He pointed at a spot to their right.

Rob turned his head and caught a glimpse of a figure in the distance, running away from them.

"Hey!" Travis called. "Come here!"

The figure wasn't completely visible through the trees, but Rob thought it slowed for a fraction of a second before running away even faster.

Travis grasped the iron bars of the fence. "Stop! Police!" But his shouts went unheeded.

"Let's go back," Paige said, already pushing aside the oak branches. "Whoever it was is gone."

"What's going on?" Gage asked, as they emerged onto the trail.

"We saw someone," Travis said. "Someone who ran when I ordered him to stop."

They hurried down the trail. Rob kept watch along the way for any sign of the fleeing man. It had been a man, he was sure, though not a big one—not someone who fitted the description Paige had given them. "Do you think the person we saw was either of the men who shot at you?" he asked, wanting to confirm his opinion.

"I don't know," she said. "I didn't get a good look. I don't even know that it was a man. Maybe it was a deer or elk or something."

"It was a man," Travis said. A slight man wearing dark clothes, not camouflage.

In the parking area, Travis stopped beside his SUV and scanned the small gravel lot. "Whoever that was must be parked up by the resort," he said.

"They could be behind CNG's gate," Gage said. "We wouldn't necessarily be able to see their car from the road."

"We'll go check."

Travis and Gage climbed into the SUV and left. Rob took Paige's arm. "Come on. Let's follow them," he said.

"We don't need to do that," she said. "Let's go back to town and wait there."

"They might need help," Rob said. He started the truck and followed Travis and Gage out onto the road.

The sheriff turned in at the entrance to CNG's property and stopped at the gate, his engine idling. He and Gage both climbed out of the SUV. Rob got out and followed them, though Paige remained in the truck. The three men looked through the bars of the gate, scanning the property, alert for the flash of sunlight on chrome or the metallic sheen of an automobile. "I don't see anything," Rob said after a moment.

"Me either." Travis studied the broken asphalt of the drive. "It's impossible to tell if anyone has driven over this recently." He studied the gate. "Though it doesn't look to me as if this chain and padlock have been moved in a while." He indicated the fine road dust sifted over the metal.

Gage looked around. "Maybe he parked somewhere near here and scaled the fence—or found a break and slipped through."

"How much farther does the road go?" Rob asked.

"Not far," Travis said. "It dead-ends in another fifty feet or so."

"Let's take a look," Gage said.

"Are we going back to town now?" Paige asked, when Rob returned to the car.

"In a minute. We just want to check the end of the road." He waited while Travis turned the SUV around, then followed him back down the drive. The sheriff had just started to turn onto the pavement when a dark-colored, older-model sedan came barreling toward them. Travis had to jerk the wheel sharply to the left to avoid being sideswiped.

Paige screamed and grabbed on to Rob, who had stomped on the brakes, narrowly avoiding a collision into the rear of the SUV. Travis brought his vehicle around and lurched onto the road, in pursuit of the vehicle, which had already disappeared around a curve.

"Hold on!" Rob said, and shot after them.

"Did you see the license plate?" he asked, as they barreled down the road.

"I didn't see anything," Paige said. Her fingers dug into Rob's shoulder as they skidded around a sharp curve. "Slow down. You're going to get us killed."

"Sit back," Rob ordered.

She released her hold on him and did so, though Rob could hear her gasps and moans each time the truck skidded in gravel or rocketed over a rough spot in the pavement. They rounded yet another curve to find a straight stretch of empty road ahead. The SUV sped up even more, and Rob followed suit, but there was no sign of the sedan.

"I hope we haven't lost him," Rob said.

"He could be anywhere," Paige said. "On a side road or in a driveway—or halfway to Junction by now. And you don't even know if he had anything to do with what happened to me."

"It seems pretty suspicious if you run when a cop tells you to stop," Rob said.

"Not everyone trusts the police," she said.

Rob said nothing, but continued to follow the sheriff's SUV. By the time they reached Eagle Mountain, Travis had slowed to the speed limit. Rob's cell phone rang and he hit the button on the steering wheel to answer it.

"We lost him." Gage's voice filled the car. "Did either of you get a look at the plate?"

"No," Rob said.

"Paige?" Gage asked.

"No," she said.

"All right. You two can go on back to Paige's place. Travis and I are going to drive around a little more. Maybe we'll get lucky and spot him."

"Will do." He ended the call and drove to the Bear's Den, where he parked in the side lot.

Paige had her door open and was out of the car and headed up the walk before he could come around to her side. "Where are you going in such a hurry?" he asked, when he caught up with her in the entryway.

"I'm going to my room."

She started to turn away, but he took her arm and turned her to face him. Her skin was the color of paste and her lip trembled, as if she was fighting tears. "Hey," he said. "Are you okay?"

"I'm fine." But everything about her, from the haunted look in her eyes to the pinched sound of her voice, said that statement was a lie. Seeing that man up there and the subsequent chase had shaken her up more than he had imagined.

"It's going to be okay," he said.

He tried to pull her close, but she jerked free from his grasp. "I'm going to lie down," she said. She almost ran down the hall, and half a second later he heard a door slam.

Rob frowned after her, debating knocking on her door and demanding that she talk to him. But he had already learned that pushing Paige was never a good idea. Later, when she came out again, he would try to get her to open up about what had her so upset.

The back door opened and Parker came in. He started when he saw Rob. "I, uh, didn't know you were still here," he said. He looked around. "Where's Paige?"

"In her room." Rob took a glass from the cabinet by the sink and filled it with water. "She's resting."

As if to prove him a liar, the door to Paige's room

opened and she came down the hall to join them in the kitchen. She ignored Rob and walked straight to Parker, grabbed his arm and shook it. "What were you doing up at Eagle Mountain Resort this afternoon?" she demanded.

Chapter Eight

Paige was counting on Rob's presence to force Parker to tell the truth about what he had been up to this afternoon. Though she had caught only a fleeting glimpse of the figure running through the trees, the punched-in-the-gut feeling that glimpse had engendered had raised her worst fears. The sight of Parker's car speeding away from them had confirmed those fears.

She shook his arm again. "Don't lie to me," she said. "I saw you."

Parker's face had lost all color. He glanced at Rob, desperation in his eyes. Rob folded his arms across his chest and leaned back against the counter. "Yes, tell us what you were doing up there."

Parker slid his arms out of the straps of his backpack and let it fall to the floor with a thud. "I wasn't doing anything wrong," he said.

"You were trespassing," Rob said.

Parker jutted his chin out. "Are you going to turn me in for that?"

Paige wondered if she was the only one who recognized the fear behind her brother's defiant glare.

"That depends," Rob said.

Parker stared at the floor, the muscles of his jaw clenching and unclenching. "I'm helping Professor Gibson with a research project," he said.

"Professor Gibson?" Paige searched her memory for the name. "The old man who helped Brenda get the grant for the history museum?"

"Yeah."

"Who's Professor Gibson?" Rob asked. "One of your instructors?"

"No, he's retired." Parker shoved his hands in the front pockets of his jeans. "But he's interested in the history of this area. He and I are trying to find the location of that World War II government research lab—the one that was developing biological and chemical weapons."

"We already determined the underground lab on the resort property isn't old enough to have been in use during the war," Rob said.

"That lab, sure," Parker said. "The professor thinks there's another one on that property."

"What makes him think that?" Paige asked.

"He's got all the declassified documents from the project, and letters and maps and stuff," Parker said. "He goes over them and finds out stuff, but he's eighty years old and it's hard for him to get up in the mountains and check stuff out. That's where I come in."

"So you were on the resort property, looking for this supposed lab?" Rob asked.

"Well, yeah," Parker said. "I told the professor about Paige seeing those two guys carrying a box into a hole in the ground, and he thought it was a good possibility. I didn't touch anything, I swear. I just walked around and looked."

"Did you find another underground chamber that could have been used as a lab?" Paige asked.

"No." His shoulders sagged again. "You came along before I could see much."

"How did you get in?" Rob asked. "The gate is chained shut."

"There's a place about two-thirds of the way along the fence line on the east side," Parker said. "Part of a big tree fell on the fence and took it down part of the way. All I had to do was shimmy up the trunk and walk right in on the fallen log."

"Why did you run from us?" Rob asked.

"Because I knew if Paige saw me, she'd have kittens," he said. "And trespassing is a violation of my parole."

Paige went ice-cold all over. She hadn't thought of that. "Promise me you won't turn him in," she said to Rob, clasping her hands together in a begging gesture. "Please." When it came to her brother, she had no shame.

He gave her a long look she found impossible to interpret. He turned back to Parker. "Did you see anyone else while you were up there?"

Parker shook his head. "Just you and Paige and the sheriff."

"Do you swear you don't know anything about the two men who fired those shots at Paige?" Rob asked.

"I swear!" Parker straightened, the color high in his cheeks. "They tried to kill my sister. If I knew anything at all, I swear I'd tell you. Why wouldn't I?"

Rob didn't answer this question. "Did you see any signs that anyone had been up there recently?" he asked. "Tire tracks or new excavation or equipment?"

"Nothing like that. But I wasn't really up there that long before y'all came around." He turned to Paige again. "You don't think the sheriff recognized my car, do you?"

"I don't think so," she said. "But Travis is really smart. You should drive my car for a few days, until this settles down."

"What are you going to do?" Parker asked Rob.

"I won't say anything to anyone," he said. "For now." He didn't look at Paige when he spoke, which was probably just as well, because she had to fight to keep from throwing her arms around his neck in gratitude. She definitely didn't want him thinking she owed him anything for this particular favor—though maybe she did.

"Thank you," she said. Then she turned to Parker. "And you tell the professor you are not breaking any more laws in the name of research. You're not even going to jaywalk across the street on your way to the campus library."

"I'm not stupid," he said.

"Then why are you acting like you are?" Paige asked.

"You can settle that debate later," Rob said. He straightened and came to stand beside Paige, facing Parker. "What has the professor learned about this World War II project?" he asked.

"A lot, I guess," Parker said. "I mean, most of it is based on that old book he used to own—the one that was destroyed before Brenda could auction it to raise money for the museum."

Rob sent Paige a questioning look.

"It was a rare book that purported to be an insider's story about the government project here in Rayford County," she explained. "Brenda's late husband had borrowed it from Professor Gibson and it was apparently worth a lot of money to collectors. One of them paid a former sheriff's deputy to destroy the book— no one has been able to figure out why."

"Right," Parker said. "But the professor has the notes Brenda took when she read the book, as well as government documents about the project that have been declassified."

"Do the documents say where the lab was located?" Rob asked.

"Not exactly," Parker said. "A lot of the documents are blacked out—all the names and stuff like that."

"Redacted," Paige said.

"What?" Parker frowned at her.

"It's called redacted, when they black out things in documents."

"Whatever. Anyway, the professor has been comparing topographical features described in a few reports with the terrain around here, and he's sure that the lab was on or near the Eagle Mountain Resort property."

"Why is he so interested in finding it?" Rob asked.

Parker stared at him. He didn't say "Duh!" but Paige was sure he was thinking it.

"Something like that would be a significant historical discovery," she said.

"Yeah!" Parker said. "And I'd be listed as one of the people who located it. I'd have an important research credit before I even graduated. It could really help me get a great job later on. Plus, it would really rock to be famous for something like that."

"What kind of things did they try to make in that lab, do you know?" Rob asked.

Parker made a face. "It was nasty stuff, that's for sure. I think the professor said they experimented with botulism and anthrax and something called Q fever."

"What about tularemia?" Rob asked.

"Yeah, I think that was on the list. Why?"

He shrugged. "Just curious."

Parker picked up his backpack and slung it over one shoulder. "Are we okay now?" he asked.

"For now," Rob said.

Parker nodded and shuffled out of the room. Paige waited until his door closed behind him, then turned to Rob. "What was all that about tularemia?"

"Didn't we already have this conversation?" he asked.

"You and Travis said you couldn't tell me anything, but it keeps coming up. Why is it so important?"

"I still can't tell you." He put a hand on her shoulder. "Trust me on this," he said. "If it had anything to do with you or with your brother, I would tell you."

"You'll keep quiet about him being at the resort today, won't you?" she asked. "I know it was a really bad decision on his part, but it wasn't criminal."

"I won't say anything," he said. "But you have to be prepared for Travis to figure it out. He's no dummy, and a good investigator."

"And he has a lot on his plate right now," she said. "I hope finding a random stranger he glimpsed for a few seconds is low on the list."

"Before we saw Parker, did you get anything out of today?" Rob asked. "Did the visit shake loose any new memories?"

"No."

"Do you think you'd recognize the two men if you saw them again?"

"I do."

"That's simple, then. All we have to do is find them."

ROB TOOK ADVANTAGE of Parker's presence at the B and B to check in with the sheriff. He was curious to know if Travis had recognized Parker, and if he had heard anything from CNG Development.

Adelaide Kinkaid sat at her usual post behind her desk in the lobby of the sheriff's department. When Rob stepped through the door the normally stern expression left her face, replaced by a smile that deepened the lines around her eyes. "Good morning, Agent Allerton," she said. "What can I do for you?"

"Good morning, Ms. Kinkaid," he said. "You're looking lovely this morning. That's a beautiful blouse you're wearing." The blouse was a purple-and-turquoise paisley print that wouldn't have been out of place at Woodstock.

Adelaide brushed her shoulder. "Oh, this old thing. I've had it forever."

Rob had a sudden image of a much younger Adelaide, a flower child with a beaded headband, dancing around at some outdoor concert in this very shirt. The idea was disconcerting, to say the least. "Is the sheriff in?" he asked.

"No. Lacy dragged him along with her to interview caterers for the wedding. You know, when I got married, my mother made a big bowl of punch and we served it with little finger sandwiches and after-dinner mints and called it good. But now brides want these big fancy dinners and dances that cost a small fortune." She leaned toward him. "Have you ever been married, Agent Allerton?"

"No."

"One of those confirmed bachelors, aren't you?" She pointed a pink-polished nail at him. "I know the type. You think you're immune to love and then one day you meet the right woman and bam!" She slammed her hand down on her desk, making him jump. "You're down for the count."

She made falling in love sound like a wrestling match. "I don't know—" he began.

"I know what I'm talking about," she insisted. "Gage was that way—such a ladies' man until Maya came along."

"Is Gage in?" Rob asked.

"No. He had to go over to the other end of the county to deal with a traffic accident. Some fool ran off the road and took out a section of Herbert Kowalski's fence. Two of his llamas got loose and Gage is having to help round them up before they cause another accident. That could take a while. Llamas can be hard to handle."

"I wouldn't know." And he hoped he never would.

She fixed her smile on him again. "Is there anything I can help you with?"

Adelaide struck him as the type to keep up with local gossip. "Have you heard anything else about what's going on up at the old Eagle Mountain Resort property?" he asked. "Has CNG revealed their plans?"

"They won't return the sheriff's calls, I can tell you that," she said. "Though my neighbor, Sandra, has a brother-in-law who works for a concrete company in Junction, and she said someone she thinks was from CNG called about getting bids to pour some building foundations. Which is interesting, considering they haven't even gotten approval from the county to proceed with any building. And I'm pretty sure the injunction that Paige's group got is still in place, and it prohibits any development on the site."

"Maybe they think they can go ahead without county approval," Rob said.

Adelaide snorted. "They'd better not try it. People here are keeping an eye on them, and if they make one wrong move, Paige and her bunch, especially, will be on them."

"They're that dogged, are they?"

"I don't always agree with her, mind you, but Paige Riddell knows how to get things done." She shook her head. "Of course, being pushy like that isn't the most attractive trait in a woman—which may explain why she's still single."

"Maybe she's choosy about who she dates," Rob said. "And I like a woman who isn't afraid to stand up for what she believes in."

"Well, I—" The phone rang, interrupting her. She held up one finger, to signal he should wait, and answered.

While Adelaide dealt with the caller, Rob wandered over to look at a series of photographs on the wall—Travis, Gage, Dwight and other officers at various community events. One photo showed Travis on horseback, leading a parade. In another, Gage was surrounded by a group of schoolchildren. Rob felt a stab of envy. DEA agents weren't normally part of a community like this. He believed what he was doing was important, but the public didn't always recognize that.

"Now, that was interesting." Adelaide had hung up the phone and looked pleased with herself. "Something you might want to know."

"Oh?" He returned to stand in front of her desk. "What is it?"

"That call was from my friend Shirley, over at the county offices. You'll never guess who is on the agenda to address the county commissioners at their meeting tonight."

He could see she wanted him to ask the question, so he did. "Who?"

"A representative from CNG Development. Apparently, he wants to present their plans for the old Eagle Mountain Resort property."

"That is interesting," Rob said. "Any idea what he's going to talk about?"

"No." She picked up her phone. "I've got to call Travis. He's definitely going to want to be there."

"Yes." Rob would make it a point to be there, too. And he was sure Paige wouldn't want to miss it.

PAIGE SURVEYED THE new front door with a critical eye. It was a darker shade of red than the old one, but she decided she liked the look. And at least she wouldn't have to explain bullet holes to her guests.

She went inside and closed and locked the door behind her. Parker was at the computer, typing away. "What are you doing?" she asked.

"While you were outside I took a call from a woman who wanted to book a room for next month," he said.

"You should have put her on hold and come and gotten me," Paige said.

"Why? I took care of it." He finished typing and looked up. "She wanted the Miner's Suite and it was available for those dates, so I took her credit card information and she's all set."

Paige came to look over his shoulder. Everything about the reservation looked right. "Thanks," she said. "How did you know what to do?" It wasn't as if she had ever shown him her system—though maybe she should have.

"It doesn't take a genius to figure out," he said.

"Even though you are smarter than the average bear." She ruffled his hair, which he hated, but he only ducked out of the way.

"What are you doing, hanging around here this morning, anyway?" she asked. "Don't you have class?"

"Not this morning."

"You're not scheduled to do a shift at the museum?"

"I told Brenda I needed to take the day off."

He avoided her gaze, which immediately set off an internal alarm bell. "A day off for what?" she asked.

"I promised Rob I'd stick around this morning and look after you. He had to go to town to do some stuff, but he didn't want to leave you alone."

"So you're my designated babysitter?"

"Hey, I couldn't exactly tell the man no, could I? I owe him."

"I'll certainly talk to him about payback when he gets here."

"Paige, don't give him a hard time," Parker said. "He's only trying to protect you. And I would have stuck around anyway, even if he hadn't asked."

"I don't need a keeper."

"Maybe not, but until those creeps who shot at you are found, you don't need to be here alone, either."

She was sensible enough to admit he was right, but the idea chafed. She was about to tell him so when the doorbell rang.

A glance through the peephole showed an attractive, sandy-haired man in his midforties, wearing sharply creased khakis and a peach-colored polo shirt that showed off a good tan, broad shoulders and a trim waist. Paige opened the door. "May I help you?"

"Are you Paige Riddell?" He held out his hand. "I'm Bryce Reed, chief financial officer of CNG Development. We own the property up on Dakota Ridge that was formerly the proposed site for something called Eagle Mountain Resort. I understand you were instrumental in halting that development."

"Yes." She eyed him warily. He seemed friendly enough, but even the friendliest person could be bent on wholesale habitat destruction. "My organization is very serious about protecting the fragile environment at that elevation," she said.

"Which is exactly what I want to talk to you about," he said. "May I come in?"

She couldn't think of a good reason to tell him

no. Parker was here with her—not that she couldn't look after herself—and she was curious to hear what Bryce Reed had to say. She held the door open wider.

"This is my brother, Parker. Parker, this is Mr. Reed, with CNG Development." The two shook hands. Then Parker stepped back and crossed his arms, tattoos and tough-guy scowl on display. Paige ignored him. "We can talk in here," she said, leading the way into the family room she used as a space for guests to hang out when they didn't want to be in their rooms.

She took a seat on a sofa and he settled into an armchair adjacent to her. Parker stood in the doorway, as if blocking Reed's escape. She scowled at her brother, hoping he would get the message that she wanted him to leave, but he ignored her and continued to glower at the CNG spokesman.

Reed either didn't notice or pretended not to. "I saw the plans Hake Development had drawn up for the property," he said. "A very ambitious project."

"A ridiculous project," Paige said. "There isn't enough water up there to support the kind of development he wanted to do, and keeping the roads clear and mitigating the avalanche danger would be a logistical nightmare. Not to mention the impact on wildlife and native trees and—"

Reed held up a hand. "You don't have to convince me, Ms. Riddell," he said. "I agree with all the points you've made. CNG has a very different use in mind for the property—one that will have much less impact."

She relaxed a little. She didn't get the impression he was trying to distract her with his charm or sell her a pack of lies. She had had enough experience with that type that she could spot them within seconds of meeting them for the first time. "I'm interested in finding out more about your plan," she said.

"I appreciate you hearing me out," he said. "What we have in mind is a small, exclusive high-altitude research facility. A few researchers and interns living on-site in the summer months in very low-profile, low-impact buildings. In the late fall we would close up the place and secure everything through the winter, and reopen when the roads are clear in late spring or early summer. No need to plow the road or worry about avalanches, no impact on elk calving season, very little traffic. We think we can use solar for much of our energy, and are looking into rainwater collection systems for our water needs, as well as compostable toilets and other green initiatives."

She let his words sink in. "It sounds almost too good to be true," she said after a moment.

He laughed—a hearty, friendly sound. "After dealing with Hake Development, I'm sure it does," he said. "I read your group's presentation of your objections against the resort development and you made some very good points. We're trying to keep them in mind as we plan this project."

"What do you want from me?" she asked.

"No wasting time with you, is there?" He smiled, fine lines popping out around his blue eyes. He really was a very attractive man. He didn't have Rob's movie-star looks, but there was something very appealing about him. Not that she trusted men in general, handsome or not. "Obviously, we'd like your support, if we can get it," he said. "I'm supposed to give a presentation about our plans to the town council this evening. I think your presence and approval of our project would carry a lot of weight with the local government."

"Now you're just trying to flatter me," she said.

"Maybe a little. But can you blame me? I think we've got a great project here—something that will make good use of the land and, incidentally, get rid of what I gather has been something of a blight on the local landscape. You've seen the property as it is now—abandoned foundations, crumbling streets, and I understand it has even attracted a criminal element. That isn't what CNG wants at all. We've already locked the gate and added additional fencing to try to keep out trespassers."

"You put a lock on a gate over the public hiking trail," she said. "I have a court order for the lock to be removed, but so far CNG has ignored it."

"This is the first I've heard about it," he said, frowning. "I wasn't aware there was a public hiking trail through the property. I'll certainly have to look into that."

"There's a public easement at one corner," she said. "The trail has been there since the late 1800s. You can't legally block it."

"I'm sure we can come to some compromise that ensures our property rights are respected as well as maintaining the public's access to the trail."

"You can either remove the gate or move the fence," Paige said. "Until you do, I can't speak out in support of this development."

She waited for his anger, but instead, he gave another smile, this one almost sheepish. "You drive a hard bargain, Ms. Riddell, but a fair one. I'll see that the gate is opened."

Paige stood, and he rose also. "I'll come to the county commissioners' meeting this evening," she said. "I'm looking forward to your presentation. And I appreciate your talking to me."

He took her hand, his grasp warm and firm. "Thanks for listening," he said.

She walked with him to the foyer, but before he could leave, the front door opened and Rob walked in. He stared at the two of them, who were still hand in hand. "Hello," he said.

Paige slipped her hand from Bryce's. "Bryce Reed, this is Rob Allerton," she said. "Rob is a guest here at the B and B. Mr. Reed is with CNG Development."

"Good to meet you." Bryce shook hands with Rob, who continued to eye him as if he suspected him of some crime.

"Are you the CNG representative who's giving the presentation to the county commissioners this evening?" he asked.

How had Rob learned that? Paige wondered. Maybe Travis had told him.

"I guess it's true what they say about word getting around fast in small towns," Bryce said. "Yes, I'm going to be talking about our plans for the property up on Dakota Ridge." He turned to Paige once more. "I'd really like to take you up to the property and show you around," he said. "I want you to see exactly what we have in mind. And I'm sure you could offer some good suggestions."

"The last time I was up there, someone tried to kill me," she said.

Maybe she had hoped to shock him a little bit with this bold statement. Clearly, she succeeded. He blinked at her, mouth half-open, eyes wide—as if he had been hit in the head with a heavy object. "Kill you? I hope you're exaggerating."

"She's not." Rob moved in closer. "Two men fired on her while she was on the hiking trail that runs alongside the fence bordering your property. Later, they came here to try to finish the job."

"Two men, you say?" He had regained some of his composure, but his affable manner of earlier was gone. "What did they look like?"

"They were big," Paige said. "They wore camouflage, almost like soldiers. But I didn't really get a good look at them."

"They drove a dark sedan and the weapon was an AR-15," Rob said.

"That is unacceptable," Bryce said. He took Paige's hand once more. "I'm so sorry you had to go through that. I had heard some criminal types had been taking advantage of what they probably saw as abandoned property. I promise you, that is going to stop now."

The fierceness of his tone—and the murderous

look in his eyes—sent a shiver through her. She withdrew her hand from his. "That's good to hear."

"If you know anything about this, you need to tell the sheriff," Rob said.

"I think I know how to handle my business," Bryce said, his voice mild, but his eyes still frigid. He nodded to Paige. "I'll see you tonight."

Rob opened the door and closed it again after Bryce had exited. He locked it, then leaned back against it, arms crossed. "What was he doing here?" he asked.

"He invited me to attend his presentation tonight," she said. "And he wants my support—well, the support of Eagle Mountain environmentalists—for CNG's plans."

"He wanted to size you up," Parker said.

She turned to her brother, who leaned back against the desk, his pose strikingly similar to Rob's. "What do you mean by that?" she asked.

"He wanted to see what the opposition looked like," Parker said. "What he was up against."

"I think Parker's right," Rob said. "He may have asked you for your support, but he really wanted to gauge what kind of a fight you were likely to put up."

"Maybe so," Paige said. "But my take is that he was being smart and trying to recruit me to his side. And he made some convincing arguments for his project."

"I think he knows something about those men who shot at you," Rob said.

"You saw the look on his face when I told him

about them," she said. "He was stunned—truly shocked."

"Maybe." Rob looked doubtful. "I think he bears watching."

"I agree," Paige said. "And I will be watching him. But I don't think he's dangerous."

Rob moved past her, pausing at her side to touch her arm and look into her eyes. "Don't underestimate him," he said, in a low voice that sent a hot tremor through her. "And don't underestimate what I'll do to protect you."

Chapter Nine

Parker consulted the map the professor had given him, and compared it to the landscape around him. The map was dotted with the crossed-pickaxes symbol that indicated the site of old mines, several of which were within the dark line that represented the boundary around CNG Development's Dakota Ridge property. "There may be others that aren't marked on here," Professor Gibson had said when he gave Parker the map. "But these are a good place to start. Locate as many as you can and report back to me."

Yes, he had promised Paige he wouldn't come back up here, but that had been fear talking. Now that he had had time to think about it, he couldn't see what harm could come from him taking another look at the property. If CNG really was going to develop the place, he and the professor didn't have much time left to make their discovery. And with everyone focused on Bryce Reed's presentation to the county commissioners that evening, Parker had figured this was a good time to finish what he had intended to do before the sheriff had interrupted him the other day.

Paige would have had a fit if she knew he was back up here, of course, but the way Parker saw it, the property was unoccupied—practically abandoned. And he was engaged in important historical research, not petty vandalism. He doubted CNG or the local cops would see it that way, so he had been careful to park his car out of sight, and to come into the property through the break in the fence, where no one could see him from the road or the hiking trail.

Rob Allerton definitely wouldn't approve of what he was doing, though he had been cool about not turning Parker in to the sheriff when he'd recognized him here the other day. Parker hadn't expected that, and it made him like the cop in spite of himself.

He still couldn't decide how he felt having the DEA agent living in the same house. Paige could pretend all she wanted that Rob wasn't interested in her, but Parker knew he was right. Was that a good or a bad thing? She needed something to focus on besides Parker. He hadn't said anything to his sister yet, but he was thinking of moving to Boulder next year and enrolling in the University of Colorado. Professor Gibson had already said he would recommend Parker for admission, and even help him get a scholarship to study history.

The professor had been a surprise since Parker moved to Eagle Mountain. The old guy had really taken an interest in Parker. It was an odd friendship— a young ex-con and a staid old professor—but Gibson was supersharp, and the two had just hit it off. The research they were doing together fascinated Parker, and the professor had helped him to see a future for himself that didn't involve menial jobs and always running from the stigma of his past mistakes.

The professor had determined that the government's secret World War II lab had been located in this area. He had unearthed accounts that mentioned a rocky ridge he thought was probably Dakota Ridge, and a nearby creek, the location of which matched up with the creek that ran along the back side of CNG's property. One letter the professor had found mentioned a view of Mount Wiley, which could be seen from where Parker was standing right now.

The problem was construction on the property had altered some of the natural terrain. Had the gully shown on the map been filled in or diverted to construct that street? Had the giant boulder indicated on the map been blasted into pieces to make room for the foundation of a house? It didn't help that Parker hadn't had much experience reading maps and orienteering, or that he had only about an hour and a half before it would be too dark to see much of anything. Where was a good GPS coordinate when you needed it?

He took a few steps toward a clearing ahead, thinking if he got out of the trees, maybe he could figure out where he was, but a loud noise startled him. Heart pounding, he hurried back into the thick undergrowth. The heavy *whump! whump! whump!* of a helicopter echoed off the rock face of the ridge behind him, growing so loud Parker wanted to cover his ears.

But he remained still, craning his neck and trying to see through the canopy of trees. He caught a glimpse of a dark shape, but that was all. Maybe just as well, since if he couldn't see the chopper through the thick undergrowth, then its occupants probably couldn't see him.

He didn't have to wait long to get a good view of the helicopter, though. A minute later, it set down in the clearing in front of him. Parker shrank farther into the underbrush as the rotors slowed, then stopped, and the roar of the engine faded. The door popped open and two men, dressed in military fatigues and carrying rifles, hopped to the ground. They scanned the area. Then a moment later, a man in a dark business suit exited the chopper. He had graying hair swept back from his forehead, and dark sunglasses perched on a crooked nose, with deep frown lines on either side of a thin-lipped mouth. He surveyed the area, then said something to the men with the guns that Parker couldn't hear.

The gunmen returned to the helicopter and unloaded a large wooden crate—about the size of a coffee table or a trunk. They set it on the ground next to the man in the suit. Stealthily, trying hard not to make a sound and scarcely daring to breathe, Parker took out his phone and began snapping photographs of the men, the box and the helicopter. He had taken half a dozen pictures when a branch cracked and a deer shot from the underbrush on the other side of the clearing.

Both men in fatigues raised their rifles and fired off a barrage of shots, peppering the deer with bullets, sending bark flying off the trunks of surrounding trees. Parker bit the inside of his cheek to keep from crying out. These guys were crazy! And he needed to get out of here as fast as he could.

The man in the suit didn't even flinch at the burst of gunfire. When the gunmen had lowered their weapons, he motioned to the crate and said something. They each took an end and headed off across the clearing, away from Parker. The man in the suit followed.

Parker waited until they were out of sight, then retraced his steps to the break in the fence, and from there to his car. His hands were still shaking as he fumbled the key into the ignition. What was going on up here?

And did he dare tell anyone about it?

WORD HAD OBVIOUSLY gotten around about that night's special guest speaker at the county commissioners' meeting, since latecomers ended up standing along the walls of the meeting room on the second floor of the Rayford County courthouse. Eagle Mountain *Examiner* reporter Tammy Patterson slid into one of the last empty seats, next to Paige, and gaped at the full house. "Most of the time Dean Eggbert and I are the only people in the audience at these things," she whispered, as she took out her tape recorder.

"Why does Dean attend?" Paige asked, picturing the short, round man whose balding head and ever-present white-shirt-with-red-suspenders combo always reminded her of the picture of Humpty Dumpty in her childhood storybook.

"His wife's book club meets at their place on Monday nights," Tammy said. "This gets him out of the house." She looked past Paige. "Hello, Agent Allerton. I heard you were back in town."

"Call me Rob," he said. "I'm here on vacation. Hoping to do some fishing."

"This meeting is called to order." The chief commissioner struck his gavel and the regular business of the commissioners proceeded, from the approval of the last meeting's minutes to authorization of funds to buy a new dump truck. Paige, who had endured her share of town meetings, struggled to keep her eyes open. Next to her, Rob sat slumped in his chair with his hands in his pockets and his chin on his chest. Paige was tempted to nudge him, to see if he was awake.

"And now, Bryce Reed with CNG Development has asked to address the commissioners."

A murmur rose from the crowd and audience members straightened in their seats as Reed, dressed as he had been that afternoon, in khaki trousers and a pastel golf shirt, strode to the microphone at the front of the room. He nodded and someone in the rear dimmed the lights, and an image appeared on the screen of a long, low building set against the familiar cliffs of Dakota Ridge.

"My company, CNG Development, wants to take a piece of land that has become an eyesore and a nuisance to this community and turn it into an important high-altitude research facility that will give back to your wonderful community rather than taking away from it," Reed said.

For the next ten minutes, he walked them through a series of before and after artist's renderings of the property, as well as bullet-pointed lists of the benefits of his proposed project—everything from green building practices to wildlife habitat protection.

"He's very persuasive," Paige whispered to Rob.

"Are you persuaded?" he asked.

"I'm reserving judgment," she said. "Companies often talk a good game, but they don't always follow through."

Reed finished his presentation and asked if anyone had questions. Seemingly everyone had a question, from Al Dawson's query about local jobs at the lab site—there would be a very small, very specialized staff, but there might be a few jobs for locals—to Merrily Rayford's concern over removing some of the dilapidated structures that were already in place on the property.

"No questions?" Rob leaned over to ask Paige.

"I'll have plenty—later. When I meet with Mr. Reed again."

Once more flashing a smile that attested to many thousand dollars of dental work, Bryce Reed closed the notebook he had brought to the podium with him. "If no one else has anything they'd like to ask—"

The door at the back of the room opened and Mayor Larry Rowe stepped in. Dressed for the office in dark slacks, white shirt and no tie, he smoothed back his graying hair and strode toward the podium. "Sorry I'm late," he muttered, as Bryce stepped aside to give the mayor access to the microphone.

"I should have known Larry wouldn't miss a chance to claim his share of the spotlight," Paige whispered to Rob.

"I just wanted to go on record as saying that the city of Eagle Mountain is one hundred percent behind CNG's proposal for their Dakota Ridge property," the mayor said. "We're pleased as can be that they're going to take something that has been a problem for the area and turn it into a facility we can all be proud of."

He looked out at the audience, as if daring anyone to contradict him.

"Thank you, Mr. Mayor," Bryce said. "I appreciate your support. And I hope in time to earn the support of many more of you."

Paige realized Bryce was looking right at her. She met his gaze with a cool look of her own.

"He thinks he's won you over," Rob said.

"As I said, I'm reserving judgment until after our meeting."

She braced herself for his argument that she shouldn't meet with Reed alone. She would let him rant for a while, then tell him she intended to take him with her. That should knock the wind from his sails. But before she had a chance to speak, a piercing siren sounded.

"That's the fire alarm." Travis, who had been seated behind them, stood. Half a dozen others in the room rose, as well. In a town with no paid fire department, the alarm was the quickest way to summon volunteers to their stations.

The room was emptying out fast when Tammy stood, her phone in her hand. "My editor just texted me," she said. "The fire is up on Dakota Ridge—at the old Eagle Mountain Resort property."

ROB STUDIED THE two bodies partially visible beneath the pile of charred timbers, illuminated by the white-hot glow of powerful LED work lights on stands on either side of the former building. The sharp scent of burning wood stung his nose, and he stood well back to avoid the rivulets of wet ash that trickled from the remains of the fire. "Any idea who they are?" he asked Travis.

"Reed says he's never seen them before—that no one was supposed to be up here." Travis glanced toward where Bryce Reed stood, talking to the assistant fire chief, Tom Reynolds.

"How did the fire start?" Rob asked. "Do we know yet?"

"Tom says he can't make an official assessment until after a formal investigation, but he's pretty sure it's arson," Travis said.

The building had been one of the few complete ones on the resort site. The eight-by-ten shed had been sided with weathered cedar and roofed with rusty metal, in an attempt to mimic an old mine shack. Rob and his team had searched the structure as part of their investigation into the underground laboratory, but found only landscaping tools and a pile of real-estate signs. The structure sat by itself, surrounded by rocky ground and broken pavement, which had kept the blaze from spreading.

"Who called in the alarm, do you know?" Rob asked.

"Jim Trotter and his wife were driving home from dinner and saw the smoke," Travis said. "They live at the end of the road here." He turned to greet the assistant fire chief, a slim, redheaded man in yellow bunker gear. "Tom, this is Agent Rob Allerton, with the DEA."

Tom shook Rob's hand.

"I was just telling Rob that the Trotters called in the fire," Travis said.

Tom nodded. "It probably hadn't been burning very long at that point, but by the time we got here, there wasn't anything we could do except keep it from spreading to the forest."

"Was the gate closed when you arrived?" Rob asked.

"Oh yeah. We had to cut the chain. The roof was caving in by the time we got the trucks over to the structure."

"And you think it was deliberately set?" Rob asked.

"We could smell the diesel fuel as soon as we got out of the truck," Tom said. "And there hasn't been any lightning. There's no electricity to the structure, so that leaves out faulty wiring."

"Any chance it was a vagrant using the shack for

shelter?" Travis asked. "Maybe they had a campfire that got out of hand."

"Anything's possible," Tom said. "We'll know more after my investigation."

"Any sign of a vehicle?" Travis asked.

"A vehicle?" Tom frowned.

"The two men who died in the fire had to get up here somehow," Travis said.

Tom looked around them, but Rob already knew there was no car or truck in sight, other than the fire and rescue vehicles and the sheriff's SUV. "I guess they could have walked in," Tom said.

"It's a long way to walk," Travis said. "And they'd have to have gear—backpacks, camping equipment, stuff like that."

"We may find what's left of it when we clear away the debris and move the bodies," Tom said. "We might even find identification on the bodies."

"What did Bryce Reed tell you?" Travis asked.

"That he didn't know anything," Tom said. "That no one was supposed to be up here. He thinks they must have climbed the fence and been squatting here and set fire to the building themselves."

"Why didn't they try to get out?" Rob asked.

"How do you know they didn't?" Travis asked.

"The way the bodies are lying." Rob gestured toward the burned-out building. "They're facing away from the door. Say an explosion caused the fire—a gas stove, or maybe they had a campfire and tried to get it going bigger by dumping some diesel on it, and the fumes ignited. It might have thrown them backward, away from the fire, but then I would think they would try to get out. Yet both of them are just lying there, next to each other."

"Maybe they were asleep," Travis said. "Or they had been drinking or doing drugs and passed out."

"Maybe," Rob said.

"Sheriff. There's something you need to see." One of the firemen, his face and yellow bunker gear streaked with soot, trotted over to them.

Travis, Rob and the chief followed the firefighter over to a rock cairn about a hundred yards from the shack, across from the remains of what had once been a paved street. "Take a look at that," the firefighter said, and pointed behind the pillar. An AR-15 was propped against the rocks. "Funny place to leave a gun like that," he said.

"Unless you wanted to make sure it wasn't destroyed in the fire," Travis said. "And you wanted it to be found." He crouched down and examined it more closely, though without touching it. "We'll leave it until the crime scene team gets up here." He turned to look back at the blackened ruins. The firefighter and the chief moved toward the fire truck parked closer to the now-open gate. "What do you think the chances are the two bodies in there belong to the two men who shot at Paige?" Travis asked.

"I didn't get a good look at them," Rob said. "And to be honest, their own mothers wouldn't know them now."

"The gun is too obvious," Travis said. "As if someone left it there to find. I'm betting when we test it, we find out it's the same gun that fired the bullets we found in Paige's front door."

The rumble of an engine and the crackle of tires on gravel announced the arrival of the crime scene van, followed by a black SUV. Two men and one woman climbed out of the van and began donning Tyvek suits and booties. The SUV parked a short distance away, and Mayor Larry Rowe got out and walked over to join Travis and Rob.

"What are you doing here?" the mayor asked Rob.

"Agent Allerton is assisting us with the investigation," Travis said.

The mayor's eyebrows rose, but he made no further comment to Rob. "What have they found out?" he asked Travis.

Rob wanted to tell the man the information was none of his business. Something about Rowe rubbed him the wrong way—though maybe that was only Paige's prejudice rubbing off on him. Clearly, she had little use for the mayor. Rob remained quiet and let Travis handle this.

"We're waiting on the investigation before we announce any results," Travis said.

A woman in white Tyvek coveralls walked over to them. "What have we got, Sheriff?" she asked.

Travis glanced at the mayor.

"You can talk in front of me," Larry said. "I know how to keep a confidence, and I think I'm entitled to be briefed about the situation."

Travis nodded, then summed up their findings for the woman—Darcy Collins, with the Colorado Bu-

reau of Investigation. "We're going on the assump-
tion this is arson, until we establish otherwise. If it is
arson, then the two bodies could be murder victims."

She nodded. "We'll find any evidence there is
to find."

Travis pointed to the cairn. "There's an AR-15 behind those rocks I want photographed and bagged for
evidence," he said.

"Got it." She signaled to her team and they began
setting small plastic flags on thin wire stakes to establish an entry and exit corridor. They strung crime
scene tape, then began photographing the burned
building and the surrounding area.

"It's pretty clear to me what happened here," the
mayor said, when Darcy had left them.

"Oh?" Rob asked.

"The AR-15 belongs to the two dead guys," Larry
said. "They were the ones who shot at Paige, up here
and at her house. They were camping out in that
shack and got careless with their fire."

"We don't know yet if this AR is the one that fired
at Paige," Rob said.

"You can test it," Larry said. "I'm sure that will
prove I'm right."

"Thank you for your input." Travis turned away.

"You'll let me know what you find," the mayor
said.

Travis didn't answer. He and Rob walked over
to Travis's SUV, where they stood in the shadowed
darkness, watching the investigators move in and
out of the glow of work lights.

Travis waited until the mayor had driven away before he spoke. "If the bodies belong to the shooter and his cohort, then we have the guilty parties and we don't need to look further," he said.

"Very convenient," Rob said. "Except we don't know why they tried to kill Paige, or what they were doing up here."

"She said she saw them carrying a big wooden crate into an underground chamber or hole or mine shaft or something like that," Travis said. "Maybe they were stashing stolen goods up here."

"Any burglaries in the area lately?" Rob asked.

"No. I can check surrounding areas. Maybe something will pop." He kicked at a rock, which rolled away down the small incline. "It's too neat. Too convenient."

"The mayor likes it."

"The mayor watches too much television."

"What does he do, your mayor?" Rob asked. "Or is that his full-time job?"

"He has a computer consulting company," Travis said. "They specialize in financial management firms."

"He's obviously a fan of CNG."

"He ran on a platform of bringing new businesses and jobs to the area," Travis said. "And he's the type who likes to have his name in the paper as often as possible. This is a hot story, so the mayor wants to make sure he's quoted."

"I've met the type," Rob said. He tried to stay far away from them. "Do you think Reed was telling the truth—that he didn't know the men or what they were doing?"

"I don't believe anyone I don't know well," Travis said.

"He came by the Bear's Den this afternoon to talk to Paige," Rob said. "He said he wanted to share his plans for the property with her and get her support."

"That sounds smart. Paige's group isn't that large, but they know how to make a lot of noise when they're unhappy about something."

"Are you saying they're troublemakers?" Rob asked.

"Not at all. They do a lot of good for the community, but they aren't subtle. They've made enemies."

"Reed asked Paige to come up here with him for a private tour. She told him the last time she was up here, someone tried to kill her. He seemed shocked to hear this. I don't think he was faking it."

"That's interesting."

"Something I thought was even more interesting—he told Paige that 'wasn't acceptable' and that he would put a stop to it."

"As if he had authority over the shooters?" Travis asked.

"Maybe. Or maybe he was just blowing smoke, trying to impress her with how powerful and in charge he was. Or maybe it was just a figure of speech. He could have meant he was going to make sure the property was secure and no one used it for criminal activity. CNG has held the position all along that they aren't responsible for anything that has happened while the property was essentially abandoned."

"I'm wondering if either of those two is the man we saw up here yesterday," Travis said.

"I don't think so," Rob said, keeping his tone casual. "I only got a glimpse, but the person we saw seemed smaller. Like a kid, even."

"What would a kid be doing up here?" Travis asked.

"Messing around. Seeing what he could find."

"He was old enough to drive," Travis said. "He almost ran us off the road. I'm going to have to talk to Paige again. I think she knows more than she's saying."

"Why do you think that?"

"Just a hunch. She was acting odd yesterday—evasive, even."

Rob started to defend Paige, then decided anything he said was going to make the sheriff more suspicious. Travis had a reputation as a shrewd and dogged investigator. Chances were, he was going to find out it was Parker who had fled from them when they were up here yesterday. Rob didn't know Travis well enough to predict how he would handle that information, but he hoped, for Paige's sake, that he would go easy on the young man.

A trio of firemen shifted the largest of the fallen timbers and the crime scene team moved in to get their first close look at the bodies. Rob didn't envy them the task. But they would want to establish the circumstances of the deaths, and secure any identification that was on the bodies before trying to move them.

"Sheriff!" Darcy raised her head and called to him.

Travis straightened and walked over to join her. Rob was too far away to overhear what she said, but he could see the scene clearly in the bright glow of the work lights. She gestured toward one of the bodies, then bent and rolled over the second one. Travis said something, then backed out of the building and returned to the SUV.

"What did she find?" Rob asked.

"Those two didn't die in the fire," Travis said.

"Why do you say that?"

"They were already dead. Both of them had been shot in the head."

Chapter Ten

Rob was eating breakfast in Paige's dining room the next morning when Travis called him. "I'm going to Bryce Reed's office this morning to talk to him," he said. "Want to come along?"

Rob pushed back his chair. "Let me check." He headed for the kitchen, but met Paige coming out. "What are you doing this morning?" he asked her, the phone tucked under his chin.

"Eagle Mountain environmentalists have a meeting at ten. Why?"

"I might need to be away for a couple of hours," he said.

"So go," she said. "I don't need a babysitter—certainly not now that those two men are dead. You said they were probably the ones who shot at me, right?"

"We don't know that for sure."

"I'll be fine." She set a bowl of fruit on the sideboard and turned back toward the kitchen. "Go."

Rob put the phone back to his ear. "Sure, I'll come

with you. Should be interesting. Where are you meeting him?"

"CNG has an office here in town," Travis said. "Come by the sheriff's office and we'll go there together."

Travis was waiting, keys in hand, when Rob arrived. "Just to be clear, I'm not here in an official capacity," Rob reminded him as they walked to Travis's SUV.

"I know. But your law enforcement connection seemed to shake Reed a little yesterday," Travis said. "I want to take advantage of that. Besides, it's always good to have another perspective."

CNG Development's Eagle Mountain offices were located in a newer strip center on the edge of town. The front room contained an empty desk and three metal folding chairs—and nothing else. Rob would have expected a file cabinet or a plant, or even pictures on the wall. Apparently, CNG wasn't too concerned about impressing visitors.

"Hello?" Travis called when he and Rob entered.

Reed, in khaki slacks and another polo shirt—mint green this time—looked out from the doorway of the office's second room. "Sheriff!" he said. "Do you have any more news about last night's events?"

"I have some information for you," Travis said. "And some more questions." He indicated Rob. "I've asked Agent Allerton to sit in with us."

"Come sit down and we'll talk." He turned to Rob. "Agent Allerton. When I met you at Paige Riddell's yesterday afternoon, you didn't tell me you were a law enforcement officer."

Reed must have been stewing about that all night, Rob thought. "It wasn't relevant," he said.

"And now it is?" Reed asked. "What interest does the DEA have in CNG?"

"Agent Allerton is assisting us with our investigation," Travis said.

Reed looked as if he wanted to argue, but he merely pressed his lips together and led them into a sparsely furnished office. He pulled up two folding chairs and took his place behind the cheap metal desk. He must have seen Travis's and Rob's skeptical looks at the budget accommodations. "We rented this space furnished, until we can construct a more permanent facility on the site," he said. He turned to Travis. "What have you found out about those two men?"

Travis took two photographs from the file folder he carried and handed them to Reed. "Identification taken from wallets found on the bodies identifies them as Joseph Welch and Dennis Petri," he said. "We'll be confirming that with medical and dental records as soon as we can obtain them."

Reed stared at the black-and-white mug shots. Travis handed Rob copies also. The photographs showed two men in their early thirties. Welch had thinning brown hair and Petri had close-cropped, curly black hair. Each faced the camera with a sullen look on his face, booking number across his chest.

"I've never seen either of them before," Reed said, and returned the photos to Travis.

"What were they doing on CNG property?" Travis asked.

"I already told you, I have no idea. They were trespassing."

"We searched the area and we haven't been able to locate a vehicle, or any personal belongings, like a backpack or camping equipment," Travis said. "How do you explain that?"

"I don't. That's up to you to investigate."

"Both men were shot in the head," Travis continued. "Do you have any idea who might have killed them?"

"Of course not." Reed managed to look indignant.

"Any theories about what might have happened?" Rob asked.

"No. It's not my job to come up with theories. These people were on CNG property illegally."

"What is it about that piece of property that attracts so many criminals?" Rob asked.

"I could turn that around and ask why this county has such a problem with illegal activity in general," Reed said.

Travis restored the photos to the folder and sat back in his chair. "Have you considered hiring a private security company to patrol the property?" he asked. "Cameras and some lighting might also help."

"We will be doing all of those things," Reed said.

"I'll be posting extra patrols in that area, also," Travis said.

Some of the stiffness went out of Reed's posture. "I appreciate that, Sheriff," he said. "But I know yours is a small department with limited staff. I would hate to take your deputies away from here in town, where they might be needed."

"Since most of the serious crime we've had lately has had some connection to that property or people involved with it, it makes sense to me to focus our efforts there," Travis said.

"From what little I know of the former owner, he was involved with some shady characters," Reed said. "The more I consider the situation, the more I believe those two men who died in the fire—and anyone else who might have been causing trouble up there before now—must be related to that. They haven't gotten the word yet that the property has new owners who have zero tolerance for anything untoward. That is going to change now, I assure you."

"I'm glad to hear it," Travis said.

"Hello? Bryce, are you here?"

Rob sat bolt upright at the sound of the familiar voice, and turned in time to see Paige in the doorway of Reed's office. Dressed casually, in a long denim skirt, boots and a long-sleeved red blouse, she still managed to convey an air of sophistication. "Oh!" She took a step back. "I didn't know you were with someone."

"Paige, come in!" Reed rose and greeted her heartily. "The sheriff and I were just finishing up."

"What are you doing here?" Rob asked, not caring if he sounded rude.

She scowled at him, but before she could answer, Reed said, "Paige and I have a lunch date."

Now her frown was for Reed. "We agreed to talk more about your plans for your research facility," she said.

"Over lunch." He came out from behind the desk. "Gentlemen, if you'll excuse me…"

"I was going to stop by and see you this afternoon," Travis said to Paige, standing also. "But if you have a minute, we can take care of my question now."

"Of course," she said.

Travis pulled out the mug shots of Welch and Petri. "Have you seen either of these men before?" he asked.

She studied the pictures for a long moment, then shook her head. "No. I don't think so."

"Could they have been the men who shot at you on the hiking trail the other day? Or who fired on you at your house that afternoon?" Travis asked.

She looked at the photos again. "I can't say these men weren't the ones who shot at me. But I can't say they are, either. I just didn't get a good enough look at them. I'm sorry."

Rob wasn't surprised at her answer. Despite her earlier assertion that she would recognize the men again, she had glimpsed them for only a few seconds, under tense circumstance. And looking at a two-dimensional mug shot was very different from seeing someone alive and standing nearby.

"That's all right." Travis put the photographs away.

"Are those the two men you found dead last night?" she asked Rob.

He looked to Travis. This wasn't his case, and he didn't know how much the sheriff wanted to reveal. Travis nodded. "We think so, yes."

"What about the gun you found last night?" Reed asked. "Can you connect it with the attacks on Paige?"

"We're waiting on ballistics tests," he said. "Interesting thing about that gun, though."

"Oh?" Paige and Reed spoke in chorus.

"There weren't any fingerprints on it," Travis said. "Whoever put it behind those rocks had wiped it clean."

PAIGE COULD FEEL Rob's eyes on her as she exited the office with Bryce Reed. Travis hadn't elaborated any more on the gun with no fingerprints, and Reed had hurried her out. But she couldn't get Travis's words out of her head. "What do you think it means, the gun being wiped off like that?" she asked as they walked toward their cars.

"My guess is the shooters wiped it every time they used it, in case someone found it." She had started toward her car, but Reed put a hand at her back and steered her toward his. "Come in my car," he said. "We'll have more time to talk."

She could have made an excuse about having to be somewhere else right after lunch, but it seemed both silly and paranoid. Reed had given her no reason not to trust him, and it was broad daylight, after all. Not to mention Rob and the sheriff were right behind them, she thought, glancing in the mirror as she slid into the passenger seat of the big SUV Reed drove.

"Would someone really do that?" she asked, as he started the vehicle. "Wipe down a gun every time he used it? And hide it in the rocks that way?"

"A guilty person might." Reed flashed her a smile. "But hey, I've never been a criminal, so I have no idea. What do you think about the Cake Walk for lunch?" he asked. "I know Eagle Mountain doesn't have that many choices, but I had breakfast there the other day and it was great. I figure the lunch will be good, too."

"The Cake Walk is fine," she said. "Did the fire last night do much damage to the property?"

"The truth is, there's not a lot up there to burn," he said. "Chances are we would have torn down that storage shed anyway." He glanced at her. "Not that I would be thanking those two for burning it down. We take trespassing very seriously and will prosecute anyone we catch up there who doesn't have proper authorization."

She shifted in her seat, thinking of Parker. She had half a mind to call Professor Gibson and read him the riot act for asking her brother to snoop around on CNG property. She would definitely warn Parker not to go near the place again.

Reed found a parking space in front of the café and they settled into a booth along one side of the cozy restaurant. Paige recognized most of the people in the room, and nodded to a few. No doubt the gossips would be busy speculating on why she was having

lunch with the local face of CNG Development—
especially since news about the fire and the discovery of two bodies up there would be all over town by
now. It might be interesting to hear some of the local
theories about that.

"You'll be happy to know I'm having the gate
across the hiking trail removed today," Reed said,
after they had placed their orders.

"I'm pleased to hear that," she said. Though the
primary purpose of the EME meeting this morning
had been to discuss their booth for an upcoming fall
festival, several people had suggested making another try at cutting the lock off the gate blocking the
trail. In the end, they had decided to wait until things
had settled down on the resort site. No one wanted a
repeat of what had happened to Paige.

"None of the people who use the trail are interested in trespassing on private property," Paige said.
"We only want to hike a trail that's a favorite of
many people around here. If you want to put a fence
alongside the trail to protect your property, we have
no problem with that, though most people who have
public right-of-way across their land settle for posting No Trespassing signs that remind people to stay
on the trail."

"We'll try the signs," Reed said. "The sheriff suggested hiring a security guard and installing cameras."

"That might not be a bad idea," Paige said.

The waitress delivered her salad and his sandwich.
"I'd really like you to come up there with me," Reed

said. "I want to take you around and show you where everything is going to be. I think you'll really like what we have in mind."

"I'd love to see it," she said. She was dying to know his plans—and she had to admit she wanted to see the scene after last night.

"I can take you up there after lunch, if you have time," he said.

She hesitated. She didn't have any guests arriving this afternoon. "As long as we're back by five," she said. "And I need to call my brother and let him know not to expect me." Parker had proved he was capable of handling any reservations that came in.

"Great." Reed grinned, then took a big bite out of his sandwich.

When they were done eating, he took care of the bill while Paige went outside to make her call. "The Bear's Den Bed and Breakfast," Parker answered, sounding very professional.

"Parker, it's Paige. I called to let you know I'll be away the rest of the afternoon. Would you mind the phone while I'm gone? I'll be back before you have to leave for work."

"Where are you going?" he asked.

"Up to Eagle Mountain Resort. Bryce Reed is going to show me around."

"You can't go up there with him," Parker said. "You don't even know the guy."

"He's a perfectly respectable businessman." She glanced over her shoulder, relieved to see that Reed hadn't yet emerged from the café. "It's broad daylight. And I'm not an idiot. It'll be fine."

"What about those guys who shot at you?"

"The sheriff thinks they were the men who were found dead up there last night."

"I don't like it," Parker said.

"I don't like everything you do, either," she said. "But we're both adults. I don't get to tell you what to do and you don't get to tell me what to do. Agreed?"

"I still don't have to like it," he said. "Just—be careful."

"I always am." She ended the call and turned to find Reed waiting behind her.

"Any trouble?" he asked.

"My brother is a little overprotective sometimes," she said. "It's sweet, really."

"I guess someone with his background knows a little too much about what the wrong kind of people will do," Reed said. He took her arm.

She stiffened. "What's that supposed to mean?" she asked. "What about Parker's background?"

"I didn't mean to offend," he said. "Someone told me he'd been in prison."

"Who told you?" she demanded.

"I don't remember—just something I heard around town. I apologize. I really didn't mean to offend you."

He looked genuinely contrite. She relaxed a little. "Parker made some foolish mistakes when he was younger, but he's working hard to get past that," she said. "I hate that some people will never let him forget his mistakes."

"Again, I'm sorry I brought it up." Reed held the door while she slid into the passenger seat, then closed it and walked around to the driver's side. "But as long as we're on the subject of the men in your life, what's your relationship to Agent Allerton?"

"He's a guest at my B and B," she said.

"I guess I read the signals wrong," Reed said. "He seemed a little overprotective of you, too."

"You must have misunderstood," she said. She was already wishing she hadn't agreed to ride with him. She hadn't expected him to question her personal life this way.

"Sorry for the nosy questions," he said. "I've devoted the last few years to my career, so I'm a little rusty when it comes to interacting with attractive women."

And what was *that* supposed to mean? "Are you married?" she asked. If he was going to ask personal questions, she might as well, too.

"Divorced. No kids. I'm a boring workaholic, though I'd like to change that. A man gets to be my age, he starts to think about the mistakes he's made."

"You're not that old," she said.

He laughed. "Maybe not. But it feels that way sometimes." He sped up when they reached the road that started the climb toward Dakota Ridge. "This is beautiful country out here," he said. "A lot wilder and more rugged than where I'm from, back east, but definitely captivating."

"Most people who live here think it's pretty much paradise," she said.

He stopped at the gates to the resort property—she couldn't help but think of it that way, even though it would never be a resort. Maybe one day everyone would call it the research campus or something similar, but until then, it would be the resort. "The fire department destroyed the lock getting to the fire last night," he said. "We'll have to fix that." He pressed a remote device clipped to the visor and the gates swung open, smoothly and soundlessly. He drove the car over the cracking pavement and parked in front of the faded sign advertising the resort. "We're going to get people in here to take all of this out," he said, indicating the sign, the broken pavement and the foundations that had never been built on. "Come on. Let's take a walk and I'll show you around."

The air held the tang of smoke, and a short distance away Paige spotted the burned-out shed, yellow crime scene tape festooning the blackened ruins. Reed saw where she was looking and took her arm. "You don't need to concern yourself with that," he said.

She pulled away from him. "Of course I'm concerned," she said. "Two people died there —men who may have tried to kill me."

"You're right. I'm sorry." He jingled his keys in his pockets. "But there's nothing we can do about that now. Will you let me show you where we hope to put the new labs?"

She followed him away from the ruins, past a Quonset hut and more crumbling foundations to a cleared expanse near the top of the ridge that over-

looked a valley filled with tall spruce and pine. "The
building would have a low profile and really blend
in with the environment," Reed said. "You shouldn't
be able to see it from the road at all."

"Where would the people who work here live?"
she asked. It was a beautiful setting. Peaceful, even,
if you could ignore the scent of smoke that lingered
in the air.

"Some would live in town," Reed said. "Although
we would have a few houses here on the property—
apartments, really, again with a low profile and very
green."

"That's good." She was only half listening to him,
her senses attuned to the woods around them. Not
even a bird sang. It ought to have been the most
peaceful setting in the world, yet she couldn't shake
a sense of foreboding.

"Let me show you where we plan to build the
apartments." He moved forward and a stick broke
under his foot with a loud pop. Paige gasped.

"It's just a stick," Reed said. "Why are you so
jumpy?"

"I guess what happened last time I was here af-
fected me more than I realized," she said.

He moved to her side and put his arm around
her. "Don't worry. I'll protect you. Here, look." He
pulled back his jacket to reveal a gun tucked into an
inside pocket.

She backed away. Knowing he was armed didn't
make her feel safer, but there was no point saying
so. Instead, she pushed down her fear and changed

the subject. "Where is the underground chamber?" she asked.

He frowned. "You mean the one where the deputy and his girlfriend were held? It's over here." He led her back to the Quonset hut, through two empty rooms to one with a dirt floor and a metal grate in the roof open to the outside air. "We may use this for storage," he said. "It could be useful having a chamber like this that's fairly well insulated."

She suppressed a shudder and forced herself to look around.

"Did you know this is where they found Henry Hake's body?" Reed asked. "They said he died of tularemia. The sheriff suggested getting the health department up here to test, but it turns out tularemia is naturally occurring and even quite common in areas of the West, so testing wouldn't prove anything."

"I didn't know that." She followed him out of the building, relieved to be in the open air again. "What do you think happened to Henry?" she asked.

"I don't know," he said. "Though he was obviously hanging out with a criminal element. Didn't his former bodyguard murder some lawyer in town? And attack the sheriff's fiancée?"

"Yes." At the time, most people had thought Ian Barnes's murder of Andy Stenson had been an isolated incident, but now she wondered if that crime was somehow related to Henry Hake's death. She looked around them, getting her bearings. "Isn't there another underground chamber?" she asked.

"Another one? I don't think so."

"The day those men shot at me, I was looking through the fence. I watched them carry a crate to a trapdoor in the earth. They went down into the ground. But it wasn't here. It was farther that way." She pointed up the ridge.

Reed took her arm. "You must be turned around. This is the only underground space—and as you saw, it was empty. You know, the terrain here can be deceptive. Instead of going into the ground, maybe they just went downhill, behind some rocks or something."

She knew what she had seen, but there was no point arguing with him. "Maybe you're right." She pulled away from him again. "I'm ready to go now."

They walked silently back to where he had parked, Paige forcing herself not to hurry. As they neared the SUV, a pickup truck sped into the drive and stopped beside them. Rob got out. "Hello, Paige," he said. "Mr. Reed."

"What are you doing here?" Reed asked.

"Parker called and asked me to check on you," Rob told Paige. "He was concerned."

Paige wanted to be upset with him for thinking he needed to look after her—but all she felt was relief. "Thanks," she said. "But he had no cause to be worried."

"That's right." Reed put his arm around her again. She could feel the gun in his jacket digging into her side. "Paige and I had a pleasant lunch, and now we're having a pleasant afternoon together."

Rob looked as if he wanted to take Reed's arm off at the elbow. "This doesn't strike me as the safest place to be, considering all that's happened up here lately," he said.

"You weren't invited here, Agent Allerton," Reed said. "You should leave now."

Paige had no desire for Rob to leave her alone with Reed again. For one thing, his insistence on continuing to touch her and hug her was giving her the creeps. She shrugged out of his grasp once more. "I need to get back to my business," she said. "Rob, could you give me a ride?" Before Reed could object, she turned her most dazzling smile on him. "Thank you so much for lunch, and for taking the time to show me your plans. I'm really pleased with what you're going to be doing with the property."

"I can take you back to town," Reed said. "I'm going there anyway."

"I don't want to keep you any longer," she said. "And Rob is going right to the B and B. Thank you again." Not waiting for a reply, she opened the passenger door of Rob's truck and climbed in.

He didn't hesitate, either, and left Reed standing alone while he climbed in the truck and backed out of the drive. He didn't say anything until they were on the road leading away from the resort property. "Are you okay?" he asked.

"Yes." She hugged her arms across her chest. "A little shaken up, maybe. I don't know what was getting to me more—remembering being shot at the other day, or the sight of all that crime scene tape around the ruins…or Bryce Reed's overly chummy manner. Did you know he was carrying a gun?"

"So am I," Rob said. "Does that freak you out?"

"No. You're a law enforcement officer. He's supposed to be a business executive."

"Maybe with everything that's happened up there, he thought he needed protection."

"Maybe. It still strikes me as odd." She shook herself, trying to dispel her dark mood. "I'm probably just being overly sensitive. There's probably nothing to worry about."

"Maybe not. But I don't trust Reed. I'm not convinced he's not part of whatever is going on up there."

She stared. "He was at the commissioners' meeting last night when those men were killed and that fire was set," she said. "And he was back east when the other crimes occurred."

"I'm not saying he pulled the trigger or lit the match," Rob said. "But I think he knows more than he's letting on." He glanced at her. "And it was very convenient to have those two out of the way, and that gun planted to link them to shooting you. A little too obvious, I think."

"I asked him about what I saw that day on the

trail—the two men carrying a heavy crate and stowing it underground," she said.

"What did he say?"

"He said I must have gotten turned around. Or misunderstood what I saw."

"Maybe he really believes that," Rob said. "Or maybe he's a very practiced liar."

She fell silent, replaying everything Reed had said to her that afternoon. She couldn't point to anything in particular that rang untrue. But she couldn't shake the feeling that something was off, either.

Rob parked at the B and B. Paige checked the time on her phone—it was after five, so Parker would have left for his shift at Peggy's Pizza. She noticed Rob scanning the area around the house before he stepped out, and he followed her up the walk to the door, vigilant.

She unlocked the door and tucked her keys in her pocket. When the door was safely locked behind them, she turned to him. "I wanted to be angry with you for following me up to the resort," she said. "But I was so glad to see you."

He pulled her to him and she did what she had been wanting to do for days now, pressing her body against his and kissing him, hard. He responded in kind, his lips claiming hers in a kiss that left her dizzy, heart pounding, craving more. He caressed her waist, then slid one hand to her hip, the other one at the back of her neck, his thumb stroking the pulse at the side of her throat in a way that had her almost purring with pleasure.

She pressed him back against the wall and began fumbling with the buttons of his shirt. Her fingers brushed at the hair on his chest and he growled against her throat, sending a shiver of pleasure running through her. A button popped off the shirt and bounced on the floor at their feet, but she ignored it. He had pulled up the hem of her blouse and splayed his fingers across her ribs, tracing the underside of one breast. She moaned, eyes closed and forehead pressed against his chest.

"Any other guests here?" he mumbled into her hair.

"No. They checked out this morning."

"Good." He slid his hands beneath her thighs and hoisted her up against him, then kissed her again. Her heart pounded so hard she imagined she could hear it.

Then she realized it wasn't her heart she was hearing—it was footsteps pounding up the walk outside. She broke the kiss and pushed at Rob. "Someone—"

But it was the only word she managed before the front window broke and flames leaped across the room.

Chapter Eleven

Rob grabbed Paige's hand and dragged her away from the spreading flames, toward the back door. He tugged his phone from his pocket as he moved and handed it to her. "Call 9-1-1," he said, and drew his gun.

Smoke was already filling the rooms, and he could hear the crackling sound of the fire spreading rapidly behind them. He eased open the back door and cautiously checked outside. No sign of anyone. Paige had reached the emergency operator and was reporting the fire, her voice surprisingly calm. He took her free hand in his and tugged her out of the house and around toward the front—in time to hear the screech of tires and catch a glimpse of a dark vehicle speeding away.

By the time they had made it into the front yard, the wail of sirens filled the air. He stared after the retreating car, swearing to himself, but a gasp from Paige made him turn around.

"My house!" she moaned, as flames leaped to the second story of the structure.

Rob pulled her close. "You're safe," he said. "Parker is safe. You can build another house."

She nodded, but he could tell she was fighting to hold back tears. She looked up at him. "What happened?"

"Someone threw a firebomb through your front window," he said. "A Molotov cocktail or something similar would be my best guess." The flames had spread so rapidly they must have been helped along by gasoline or some other fuel.

She shuddered. "Who hates me so much?"

He put away his gun so that he could wrap both arms around her. "I don't know," he said. "But I won't give up until I find out."

She fumbled at his chest, and he realized she was doing up the buttons on his shirt—the ones that were left, anyway. "You probably want to, um, straighten up before the firefighters get here," she suggested.

He took over buttoning the shirt and tucking it into his pants. "I'm sorry we were interrupted," he said.

But she didn't answer, her gaze fixed on the sheriff's department SUV pulling in across the street, followed by an Eagle Mountain Volunteer Fire Department pumper and ladder truck. The firefighters poured out of the vehicles and went to work right away. Rob and Paige walked out to meet Gage, who was just getting out of the SUV.

"What happened?" he asked. He scowled at the burning house. The flames were already licking at the roof.

"Someone threw something through the front window," Paige said. "In broad daylight."

A second SUV parked behind Gage's, and Travis climbed out. His fiancée, Lacy Milligan, got out of the passenger side. Lacy hurried to Paige and embraced her. "Travis and I were headed to his folks' place for dinner when the call came in," she said. "I'm so glad you're okay."

"Rob says this wasn't an accidental fire," Gage said, as Travis joined the two men, a short distance away from the women.

"Paige and I were in the front hall when someone threw a firebomb through the front window," Rob said. "The flames spread immediately. We went out the back door and got to the front in time to see a car speeding away."

"You were in the front hall?" Travis asked. "Had you just come in, or were you going out?"

"We had been out and hadn't been home long." No point in mentioning they had been making out. They had been moments away from doing it up against the wall.

"Paige had lunch with Bryce Reed," Travis said.

"Right," Rob said. "And after that, he took her up to the Dakota Ridge property to show her around. Parker was worried about her and called me, so I drove up there to make sure she was all right. She elected to ride home with me."

"Why would she ride with you instead of coming back with Reed?" Gage asked.

"You'd have to ask her that."

"I'm wondering about the timing," Travis said. "Was someone watching the house, waiting for Paige to come home so they could throw that firebomb? Or did they even know she was home?"

"Reed would have had a good idea about how long it took to travel from his property to the B and B," Gage said.

"A firebomb doesn't seem like his style," Rob said. "And the car I got a glimpse of wasn't his. I'm betting if you question him, he'll have an alibi to prove he wasn't anywhere near Paige's place this afternoon."

A battered Toyota pulled in behind the sheriff's department vehicles and Parker got out. Leaving the driver's door open, he ran to them. "Paige! Peggy told me she heard there was a fire here? Are you okay? What happened?"

Paige hugged her brother. "I'm okay." She glanced over her shoulder at the fully engulfed house. "I'm sorry, but anything you had in there is gone. We didn't have time to save anything."

"I've got my laptop and most of my schoolbooks in the car," he said. "But what happened?" His arm still around Paige, he addressed this last question to Rob.

"Someone threw a firebomb in the front window," Rob said.

"Who?" Parker demanded.

"We don't know," Travis said.

"Do you have any ideas?" Gage asked. "Anybody mad at you for anything?"

"No!" Paige answered before her brother could speak. "Why would you think this has anything to do with Parker?"

"*Does* this have anything to do with you?" Travis asked, addressing Parker.

"No," he said.

"The B and B is my business," Paige said. "Whoever did this wanted to hurt me."

"Parker lives there," Gage said. "Even if he's not involved in anything illegal now, he might have friends from his past who think he betrayed them, or have some other reason to want to get back at him."

"No." Parker shook his head. "I don't even know anyone like that. I was a small-time addict and a petty thief." He looked to Rob. "You know my case. Tell them this doesn't have anything to do with me."

"He's right," Rob said. "I don't think this is connected to Parker."

Travis turned to Paige. "Then what have you done that has someone so upset?" he asked.

"I wish I knew," she said.

"What is your environmental group up to these days?" Gage asked. "Are you involved in any more lawsuits?"

"No," she said. "Nothing like that."

"None of this is Paige's fault," Lacy said. "It's the fault of whoever threw that firebomb."

"We're just trying to figure out what's going on," Travis said. "Knowing who might have a motive for wanting to harm her could help."

"I haven't done anything to anyone," she said. "I

even agreed to support CNG Development's plans for the Dakota Ridge property."

"That must have made Bryce Reed happy," Rob said.

"It's not as if my support means anything," she said. "I imagine the county is thrilled to see the property put to good use. Right now it's an eyesore. The research lab CNG is proposing will at least bring in some tax money and maybe even a few jobs."

"What about your ex-husband?" Rob asked.

"What about him?" Her eyes met his, her expression defiant.

"You said he wasn't a very nice man. Would he try to hurt you this way?"

She shook her head. "I haven't talked to him in years. I was so grateful to get away from that marriage that I let him keep most of the money and property." She glanced at the burning house again. "I bought this place with money an aunt willed to me."

"You can rebuild," Lacy said. "Better than ever. You have a lot of friends here in town who will help."

Assistant fire chief Tom Reynolds crossed the lawn to join them. He removed his helmet and wiped sweat from his forehead. "I'm sorry, Paige, but we weren't able to save the house. It went up so fast, I have to think it had some help."

"Someone threw a firebomb through the front window," Rob said.

Tom nodded. "I'm sorry to hear that, but knowing that will help my investigation."

"Thank you for keeping the fire from spreading," Paige said. "I know my neighbors appreciate it."

"Second arson in twenty-four hours," Tom said. "Think we have a firebug in town, Sheriff?"

"I don't know," Travis said. "We'll be looking for any connection."

"The fire's under control," Tom said. "But we're going to be here for a while, until we're sure everything's cold. I'll give you a report when I have one from my investigator."

"Thanks, Tom," Travis said. He turned to Paige and Parker. "Do you two have somewhere to stay?" he asked.

"I can stay with Professor Gibson," Parker said. "He's already made the offer for me to stay at his place anytime, and it'll make it easier to work on our research project."

"Paige can stay with me at my parents' place," Lacy said.

"Rob was staying at the B and B, too," Paige said.

"Don't worry about me," Rob said. "I'll get a room at the motel." Their eyes met. He wanted to pull her close, to comfort her and tell her everything would be all right—but that didn't seem appropriate right now, with an audience.

She leaned forward and squeezed his hand. "Thank you for getting me out of there safely," she said. "I was in such shock, I'm not sure I could have moved."

"I'll be in touch," he said.

"I guess I'd better get back to work," Parker said.

"Peggy let me come over here when we heard the news, but I don't want to leave her in the lurch."

"Go on," Paige said. "I'll be fine."

"She will be," Lacy said. "Do you have your car?"

"I left it at CNG's offices this afternoon," she said.

"We can walk over to Mom and Dad's and get my car," Lacy said. "Then I'll take you to get yours." She frowned. "That is, if you have your keys."

"My keys are in my pocket." Paige patted her skirt.

"I'll call my folks and let them know we're not going to make it to dinner," Travis said.

Paige cast a last look at Rob, then let Lacy lead her away. Parker drove off, and Gage left in his cruiser. Travis turned to Rob. "Any ideas?" he asked.

"I'm thinking Paige saw something—or someone thinks she saw something—up at the resort property the day she was shot at."

"The two men who shot her are probably dead," Travis said.

"They may have been the ones to fire at her, but maybe they were acting on the orders of someone else."

"Who?" Travis asked.

"I don't know. Maybe the same person who killed Henry Hake. I think it has something to do with that property, but I can't figure out what. I'm going to do a little deep digging of my own."

"Let us know what you find out," Travis said.

"I will." And then he was going to go after whoever was making Paige's life such hell, and make them wish they had never crossed her.

MR. AND MRS. MILLIGAN were happy to have Paige stay in their guest room. "Stay as long as you need," Jeanette Milligan said. "I'm so sorry about your home and business. I hope you'll be able to rebuild soon."

"As soon as possible," Paige said. Even so, she would lose months of business. She would probably have to find other work to pay her bills. She had money in savings, but she didn't want to exhaust that.

"Do you mind if I give you a little unsolicited advice?" Lacy asked, as she and Paige walked out to Lacy's car.

"Go ahead," Paige said.

"It's easy to get overwhelmed when something horrible happens," she said. "What has helped me is to focus on what is right in front of me at the moment— what I have to do in the next hour. You have a little control over that. Trying to think much further ahead than that can be too much."

"Is that how you survived when you were wrongfully convicted of killing your boss and sent to prison?" Paige asked. She still had a hard time imagining the sunny, stylish woman in front of her living in a women's prison.

"It is," Lacy said. "Now that I'm in a better place, I can afford to think about the future more, but back then, I stayed focused on the now. It helped."

"The future like your wedding to Travis." Paige

welcomed the chance to change the subject. "How are the plans coming?"

"They're going great."

All the way to CNG's offices, the two women talked wedding gowns, wedding cakes and wedding decorations. Lacy's happiness was contagious, and life seemed less bleak by the time Paige stepped out in the parking lot of the strip center to claim her car.

The door of CNG's office opened and Bryce Reed stepped out, followed by Mayor Larry Rowe. "Hello, Paige," Reed said.

"Are we interrupting something?" Paige asked, addressing her question to the mayor.

"The mayor and I were discussing groundbreaking for the new research facility," Reed said. "We want to make it a real event, with a barbecue, balloons for the kids, maybe even some games."

"You don't have approval from the county yet, do you?" Paige asked.

"With the mayor behind us, and your support, we shouldn't have any problems," Reed said.

The mayor said nothing, merely glowered at the two women and moved past them toward his SUV. Apparently, Paige's support for his new pet project wasn't enough to make him forgive her for past sins.

When the mayor had driven away, Reed said, "I was wondering if you'd forgotten about your car. I thought it would be gone before I got here, since you left the Dakota Ridge property before I did. You know I would have been happy to give you a ride back here to your car. You didn't have to run off."

She wasn't going to defend herself to this man, who at the moment sounded more like a whiny little boy. "Someone firebombed my house this afternoon," she said. "Do you know anything about that?"

"What?"

"Someone set my house on fire," Paige said.

"Paige, that's horrible." He rushed forward to take her hand. If he was faking his shock and concern, he was doing an Emmy-worthy job of it. "Are you all right? Is the damage very bad?"

"It's gone—everything I own and my business with it." Her voice shook, and she fought hard to keep back tears—tears of both sorrow and rage. "Do you know why anyone would do something like that to me?"

He took a step back. "I'm really sorry to hear that," he said. "But why would I know anything about it?"

Was he really as innocent as he looked? "Nothing bad happened to me until that day I was hiking and looked over onto your property and saw those two men, and they saw me," she said. "Since then, it's been one horrible thing after another."

"I can see how the timing seems suspicious to you," he said. "But from what I know of you and your efforts with the Eagle Mountain environmentalists, I think it's not unreasonable to believe that you're a woman who has made enemies in her life. But I'm not one of them."

Lacy touched her arm. "Maybe we should leave," she said softly.

"Yes." Paige walked to her car. Lacy went with her.

"Maybe the best thing to do would be to avoid anyone from CNG until things cool off," Lacy said. "If they do have something to do with the threats against you, there's no sense making them angrier."

Paige nodded. "You're right. I shouldn't have taken my anger over all this out on Reed." She glanced toward the office, but the door was shut now, with no sign of Bryce Reed.

"It's understandable." Lacy rubbed her back. "When we get back to the house, why don't you take a hot bath and try to relax? I'll find some clothes for you to change into."

Paige realized the clothes she was wearing smelled of smoke from the fire. A hot bath did sound relaxing, but she didn't want to go to Lacy's house—not yet. She pulled her keys from her pocket. "Is it all right with you if I come to the house later?" she asked. "I'd like to drive around for a while—do some thinking and clear my head."

"Of course," Lacy said. "You'll be careful, won't you?"

"I will. I promise." She got into the car and waited until Lacy had pulled out of the lot before she drove out behind her. When Lacy turned off toward her parents' home, Paige kept going, all the way to the motel out by the highway. She drove around the lot until she spotted Rob's truck; apparently, the fire hadn't spread to the parking area beside her house and reached his vehicle.

She studied the row of rooms facing the parking area, then slipped her cell phone from her pocket and dialed his number. "Can I come see you?" she asked when he answered.

"Of course," he said. "Where are you now?"

"I'm right outside."

She waited, and in a few seconds, the door to one of the rooms opened and he stood there, dressed only in jeans, the phone in one hand. She got out of the car and went to him. When he pulled her into his arms, and into the room, it felt exactly like coming home.

Chapter Twelve

Rob let Paige lead the way, letting her show him what she wanted—what she needed. If she wanted comfort, he would do his best to comfort her. But as she wrapped herself around him and her lips claimed his, he realized she was picking up where they had left off at the B and B—finally letting down her guard and giving in to the passion that had sizzled between them since he had moved in under her roof.

She broke off the kiss and leaned back a little in his arms, her gaze sweeping over him, assessing. "Nice," she said, the single word sending heat through him. She planted a kiss in the center of his chest, and smoothed her hands over his stomach, stopping at the snap of his jeans. His erection strained against the fly, and when she dragged her nails over it, he shuddered.

Her eyes met his. "I hope you have protection," she said.

"I do."

"Oh?" She looked amused. "Awfully sure of yourself, aren't you?"

He gripped her waist, pulling her tight against

him. "Paige, that firebomb wasn't the only thing burning in your house and you know it." He slid his hands up to cradle her head. "I've wanted you from the first day I saw you, in the hallway at the courthouse."

She blinked. "I was terrible to you that day. I accused you of not knowing how to do your job."

"Yeah, and I didn't like that one bit. But if you could have seen yourself—so beautiful and fierce and doing everything you could to stand up for your brother. I had to admire that."

"So angry women turn you on?" She slid her hands around to cup his bottom.

"No. But you turn me on."

"That first day, sex was definitely not on my mind," she said. "But you've grown on me." She reached down and started to lower his zipper, but he stopped her, then began undoing the buttons of her blouse. He pushed the fabric off her shoulders and paused to admire the full breasts swelling above the lace of her bra before reaching around and unfastening this garment and tossing it aside also.

She gasped when his lips closed over her nipple, and squirmed against him in a way that made his vision momentarily blur. He grasped her hips, stilling her, and transferred his attention to her other breast. At the same time, he lowered the zipper of her skirt and pushed it and her underwear down, until they puddled around her ankles.

He began kissing his way down her body, her skin soft and warm beneath his lips. When he lowered himself and put his mouth over her sex, she cried out and dug her fingers into his shoulders. He closed his eyes and his senses homed in on the taste and scent of her, the feel of her hands on him and his own desire building within him. All he wanted and needed right now was to be here with her, to give her as much pleasure as he was able.

She squirmed against him, her breath coming in gasps. He looked up, transfixed by the passion playing across her face. Being able to make her forget, at least for this little while, her fear and loss made him feel ten feet tall and bulletproof. She was the most precious thing in the world to him in that moment, worth every bit of aggravation she had ever caused him.

She came with a cry of triumph, and he rose to catch her in his arms, gathering her up and carrying her across the room to the bed, where they fell together, entwined.

Paige reveled in the feel of Rob's body against hers—all warm muscle and masculine strength, his every touch both tender and insistent. They stripped each other of the last of their clothing, and then he fumbled in the plastic shopping bag on the floor beside the bed and came up with a condom packet. Watching him sheathe himself with it left her breathless and trembling, but instead of pushing her down on the bed and kneeling over her, he lay back against the pillows and beckoned to her.

"What do you want?" she asked, grinning.

"The question is, what do *you* want?" He pulled her up on top of him and looked into her eyes.

She felt stripped of more than clothing beneath that gaze. He made her want a lot of things she had told herself for years that she didn't really need—companionship, protection, even love.

She kissed him, long and hard, then positioned herself over him and let him fill both her body and her spirit. They moved together, led by instinct and pleasure. They kept their eyes open, watching each other, seeing passion and trust reflected back. Their movements grew faster and more intense, and she felt herself losing control. But instead of holding back, she gave herself up to the moment, and a second, deeper climax overwhelmed her, even as he found his release beneath her.

They clung together for a long time afterward, her head on his chest, his arms wrapped around her, his sex still inside her. Then, with a long sigh, he rolled them to their sides and slid out. He discarded the condom, then lay back down, pulling her to him once more. "I'm glad you came to find me," he said, stroking her hair. "I wanted to go after you when you left with Lacy."

"She took me to get my car. Then I told her I needed to drive around and think."

"And you drove here." His gaze held the unspoken question—*why?*

"You're the person I wanted to be with," she said. "To tell you the truth, that surprises me—and frustrates me a little, too. I've worked so hard to be independent, it's hard for me to lean on someone else."

"I'm not going to confine you, Paige," he said. "I meant it when I said I appreciated how strong you are. I don't want to change that. But even the strongest nation in the world needs allies. Let me be yours."

She rested her head on his shoulder again, in that warm hollow where she fitted so perfectly. "I'm happy to have you as my ally," she said.

His arm tightened around her. "Does it upset you to talk about what happened this afternoon?"

"I think it might help, actually," she said. "Talking, I mean. Or at least, having you listen."

"Did you run into any trouble when you went back to CNG's office?" he asked.

"Bryce Reed came out of his office when Lacy and I showed up to get my car. The mayor was with him."

"I got the impression the two were pretty cozy on this project," Rob said.

"Larry still isn't speaking to me," she said. "He's never going to forgive me for opposing the original development. Not that I'm losing sleep over it."

"What about Reed?" Rob asked. "What did he say?"

"It's not so much what he said as what I said." She winced, remembering. "I kind of went off on him. I accused him of knowing something about the fire, and about the men who shot at me. He denied it, of course, and I felt bad afterward."

Rob massaged her shoulder. "Don't be so quick to mistrust your instincts," he said. "I can't prove Reed had anything to do with what happened today, but I'm going to be watching him closely. Everything seems connected to that property on Dakota Ridge. CNG owns the land, so how could Reed not be aware of what is happening up there?"

"I think I'm going to let you worry about that, while I focus on rebuilding my business." *And my life*, she silently added. She kissed his neck and sniffed. "You smell like smoke."

He kissed the top of her head. "So do you," he said. "I was getting ready to take a shower when you showed up."

"A shower sounds good. Is it big enough for two?"

"For two people who really like each other."

"Then why don't we give it a try?"

"I like the way you think."

PAIGE LEFT ROB'S hotel room well after dark, after she had called Lacy and apologized for being absent so long. Rob hadn't tried to persuade her to stay, sensing that she wanted a little space between them to think about what had happened. So they'd parted with a kiss and a promise to talk again the next day. He slept fitfully, the smell of her clinging to the sheets and disturbing his dreams. Paige Riddell was a complex woman who promised to complicate his life considerably. But he had been taking the easy road when it came to relationships for all his adult life. Maybe it was time he tried a different, more challenging path.

He rose early, in time to call his Denver office before his boss reported for work. As he had hoped, the admin, Stacy, answered the phone. "Are you calling to tell us you're cutting your vacation short and coming back to work early?" she asked. "Because we're swamped."

"No," he said. "I'm calling to ask if you can do me a little favor."

"I thought you were supposed to be fishing," she said.

"I am—just not always for trout."

"What do you want me to do?" There was no mistaking the suspicion in her tone.

"I want you to do a little background check on a guy named Bryce Reed. He's chief financial officer of an outfit called CNG Development."

"Is this related to a case you're working on?" she asked.

"Peripherally."

"Is that a fancy way of saying no?"

"I just want a little history on the guy, and to know if he has a record," Rob said.

"The boss won't like it."

"The boss doesn't have to know."

The silence on the other end of the line was so long, he wondered if she had disconnected. But at last she said, "True. As long as you're on the right side of the law."

"I promise I'm one of the good guys. And I'll bring you a box of Godiva chocolates for your trouble."

She laughed. "I'm not too sure you are a good guy, but I'm not going to pass up good chocolate. I'll run this guy and let you know what I find."

"Thanks."

He ended the call and checked the time—8:45. Too early to call Paige, who had had a rough day yesterday. Too early to drive out to the CNG offices and watch Bryce Reed.

Someone knocked on his hotel room door, and his heart sped up. He hurried to check outside and felt a little foolish when he saw that his visitor wasn't Paige, but Parker. "How did you know this was my room?" he asked, after he had opened the door.

Parker shrugged. "I saw your truck and figured I'd knock on doors until I found you. It's not like the motel is that big."

"What can I do for you?" Rob asked.

"Can I come in?"

"Sure." He stepped aside and the young man moved past him. He sat in one of the two chairs at the small table in front of the window, and Rob sat across from him.

Parker was wearing the same black T-shirt he'd had on the day before, and the same jeans, though he had shaved and smelled of soap.

"Everything go okay with the professor last night?" Rob asked.

"Yeah. He's cool." He shifted in his chair and looked around the room—everywhere but at Rob.

"What can I do for you?" Rob asked again.

At last Parker's gaze met his. "I want to help find out who is doing all this stuff to Paige," he said.

"How can you help?" Rob asked.

"I don't know. But two people are better than one, right?" He ran his hand through his short hair. "I just don't want to stand around doing nothing while someone tries to hurt her again," he said.

"Any ideas who that someone might be?" Rob asked.

Parker frowned. "I was up on Dakota Ridge again the evening after that day you and Paige and the sheriff saw me." He held up his hand. "I know I promised I wouldn't trespass up there again, but this was important. If I was going to find that World War II lab, I had to do it before CNG broke ground on their new research facility. After that, the place will be crawling with construction crews."

"You were there the evening those two men were killed?" Rob asked. "And you're just now saying something?"

"I didn't see anyone killed," Parker said. "And I don't know anything about the fire, either. But I did see some strange stuff while I was up there. Maybe it doesn't have anything to do with Paige, but what if it does?"

Rob studied the younger man. Parker's shoulders were slumped, but his expression was that of a man refusing to accept defeat. "Why come to me instead of the sheriff?" he asked. "I don't have any official role in this case."

No fidgeting this time. "You heard the questions

Sheriff Walker was asking me yesterday. He already thinks I might have something to do with all of this."

"I think the sheriff is trying to look at this from all angles and cover all the bases," Rob said. "He's being a good cop."

Parker's look of disdain said he didn't believe "good" and "cop" should be used in the same sentence. "You didn't turn me in to him after you saw me up at Dakota Ridge that day," he said.

"Maybe I was just trying to impress your sister."

"I figured that was a given. But you wouldn't be the worst thing that ever happened to her."

Rob definitely hadn't expected that, and had to resist the urge to ask Parker to elaborate. But now wasn't the time. "What did you see up on Dakota Ridge?" he asked.

"A helicopter. One of those little ones, like a traffic copter or something. Only this one was very sleek and expensive looking. I heard it coming and ducked into some really deep undergrowth. I figured it was a medical chopper, or maybe military, and would fly over. Instead, it landed right there in the middle of what used to be a street. The door opened and these two guys in camo fatigues, with AR-15s, jumped out. Then a man in a business suit followed them."

Rob sat forward, alert and intrigued. "What did they do?"

"The guys with the guns unloaded a wooden crate from the helicopter, while the guy in the suit watched. There was a pilot, too, but he never got out."

Paige had mentioned seeing two men carrying a

wooden crate that day on the hiking trail. "What did they do with the crate?" Rob asked.

Parker shook his head. "I don't know. About that time a deer wandered out of the woods. One of the guys with the guns whirled around and fired on it—just about cut it in half. Totally freaked me out. All I wanted to do was get out of there as fast as I could. I crept back in the woods, as quietly as I could. It was probably only five minutes, but it seemed like forever until I was over the fence, and maybe another fifteen before I got to where I had parked my car, in the woods about a quarter mile back toward town."

"What time was this?" Rob asked.

"It was early. The commissioners' meeting started at six thirty, and this was before then, but not too far ahead of time—maybe six o'clock."

"What time did you leave?"

"It was six forty when I got back to my car."

The fire had been called in at seven thirty. "The crate sounds like the one Paige saw," Rob said. "Similar, at least. Did you recognize any of the men?"

"No. But I have pictures." He took his phone from his pocket, swiped through a few screens, then turned it toward Rob. "I was back in the woods a ways, and I was so nervous I was shaking, but maybe if you blow them up or work some magic in a photo lab…"

Rob stared at the blurry photograph of two men in fatigues and one in a suit, standing by a helicopter. Their faces were too indistinct to make out.

"There's more, if you want to flip through," Parker said.

The next image was a closer shot of the man in the suit. The third picture was zoomed in even closer. Though still not distinct, the photograph did make one thing clear.

"This isn't Bryce Reed," Rob said. And he didn't think the men in fatigues were either of the ones who had been killed and left to burn in the shack.

"No," Parker agreed. "I never saw this guy before in my life."

Chapter Thirteen

Paige spent much of the next day canceling reservations, helping people find new accommodations, dealing with the insurance company and transferring money from savings to pay her ongoing bills. Later, she would need to go shopping, to replace at least a few of her necessities, and she would need to start hunting for a place to live.

She hung up the phone after yet another call and stared out the window of the guest bedroom where she was working. Lacy and her parents were warm and gracious hosts, who lent her clothes and toiletries, and didn't ask questions about where she had been until late the night before, but Paige couldn't stay here long-term. She wasn't comfortable being an unexpected guest, and though the Milligans weren't at all intrusive, she valued her privacy.

She resisted the urge to call Rob. He was probably working, and the last thing she wanted was for him to think that one night of incredible sex had turned her clingy. She had decidedly mixed feelings about getting involved with the lawman. On one hand, he had been a rock at a time when everything else in her world was unsteady. He was a lot smarter—and a lot more compassionate—than she had given him credit for. He liked—or at least he said he liked—her independence. And yes, the sex had been pretty incredible.

But he wasn't going to stay in Eagle Mountain, and she had no intention of changing her life for the sake of a man ever again. And who was to say all these warm feelings between them hadn't been generated by her current crises situation? When life settled down again, they might turn out to hate each other. Better to not let herself get too emotionally invested until she knew for sure.

She closed the notebook she had been using to keep track of all her tasks and went downstairs. She needed to get out and clear her head, so she took a walk downtown, and ended up at the Eagle Mountain History Museum.

Brenda Stenson looked up from behind the front counter when she entered. "Paige!" Brenda came out to envelop her in a hug. "I heard about your B and B. How horrible for you."

"Yeah, well, I figured I'd see if you had any advice for me when it came to rebuilding." Brenda's own house had been destroyed by an arsonist earlier in the summer. That man had been caught, but what were the odds of two women being the victims of intentional fires in such a short period of time, in such a small town?

"I can tell you plenty of things not to do," Brenda said.

"Such as?"

"Such as don't decide to build something completely different from the original house and expect the insurance company to just hand over the check," she said. "I had to threaten to take my insurer to court, and jump through dozens of hoops, before they finally agreed I could build a triplex in place of my original single-family home."

"I drove by the site the other day and it looks as if things are coming along nicely," Paige said.

"They are—finally. And I have a waiting list of potential renters."

"I guess this means you won't be moving back into one of the units?" Paige asked.

"Dwight and I prefer his cabin on the ranch."

"I'm happy for you." Paige was telling the truth. Brenda had suffered through a lot since her husband, Andy, had been murdered, and she deserved all the happiness she had found with Deputy Dwight Prentice. But Paige wasn't in the same situation as Brenda. "Too bad your rental units aren't already finished," she said. "I'm going to need some place to live until my house can be rebuilt. From everything I heard this morning, it could be a year or more before I'm ready to open for business."

"Oh, Paige, I'm so sorry." Brenda leaned over and

squeezed her hand. "What will you do in the mean-time?"

"I'll have to find a job. Not a lot of those around, either."

"Maybe you could find another house to run as a B and B," Brenda said.

"I thought of that. But I'd never be able to swing the loan, not when I still have a mortgage on the Bear's Den." Those payments would have to continue to be made while the house was being rebuilt. "I've got a business degree and experience running my own business," she said. "I'll find something."

"When you're ready, I can put you in touch with my contractor," Brenda said. "And if you have any questions about permitting or zoning, I feel like I'm becoming a local expert on those topics."

"Thanks," Paige said. "That's not the only reason I stopped by this afternoon. I wanted to ask you about Professor Gibson."

"Oh?" Brenda looked surprised. "What about him?"

"Parker is staying with him until I can find a place for both of us," she said. "And they're working together on some kind of project involving that secret World War II laboratory that was supposedly located in the county."

"That's right," Brenda said. "You can blame me for getting the two of them together. I heard the professor was interested in digging into the history of the lab and I knew Parker would be the perfect person to help him. From what Parker tells me, they've really hit it off."

"I guess so," Paige said. "I just worry about Parker getting into trouble, trespassing on private land or poking his nose where he shouldn't while trying to find this lab. And wasn't the government working on some really dangerous stuff there? What if he finds it and is exposed to some horrible disease?"

"I wonder if that's what happened to Henry Hake," Brenda said.

"I heard a rumor he died of tularemia," Paige said.

Brenda nodded. "The rumor is true. And the professor tells me tularemia is one of the things the government was working on in that lab."

"But the underground space where they found Henry Hake wasn't the World War II lab," Paige said.

"No, it wasn't." Brenda shrugged. "Maybe it's just a weird coincidence. Do you want me to put a bug in the professor's ear about making sure Parker plays it safe? He and I have gotten to be pretty good friends since he took an interest in the museum."

"I'd appreciate it," Paige said. "But make sure he doesn't know it came from me. Parker already thinks I meddle in his life too much."

The bell on the door rang as a couple with two elementary school–age girls entered. Paige excused herself and went back outside. Her phone rang as she was crossing the street—a number she didn't recognize. When she answered, she was surprised to hear Bryce Reed's voice.

"Paige. I'm glad I caught you," he said. "How are you doing?"

"I'm coping." The best answer she could think of, considering all that had happened.

"I'm calling to invite you to a press conference at our Dakota Ridge property tomorrow morning," he said. "We're going to officially unveil our plans for the site and I'd love to have you there."

So he hadn't really been calling to see how she was doing. She couldn't decide whether to be annoyed at his lack of concern or relieved. "So the county commissioners have approved your plans?" she asked.

"Oh, they will," he said. "We've heard only good things from that quarter. This is to get the public excited about what we're going to be doing. Will you be there?"

"I'll try to make it," she said. "What time?"

"Ten o'clock. I'll save a place for you."

He disconnected before she could tell him she wasn't going to be CNG's pet environmentalist, but decided that was her bad mood talking. She would go to the press conference tomorrow, if only for a chance to have another look at the property.

PAIGE WAS WAITING on the front porch when Rob arrived to pick her up for dinner that evening. As he made his way up the walk, he felt a little like a teenager, picking up his date from her parents' house. The full-skirted, flowered dress she wore added to the retro feel of the moment. He took a chance and kissed her cheek in greeting. "How are you doing?" he asked.

"All right." She smoothed the skirt of the dress. "Lacy loaned me this. It's a little frillier than I usually go for."

"It looks good on you," he said. He glanced toward the door. "Should we go inside and say hello?"

"Lacy and her folks are having dinner at Travis's family ranch. They asked me to come, too, but I think they were relieved when I told them I had other plans. They've been great about respecting my privacy."

Maybe that was because Paige was the type of woman who gave off very clear warnings for others not to get too close. Which made him feel especially privileged that she had let down her guard with him. "Where would you like to go for dinner?" he asked.

"Would you mind if we stayed here?" she asked. "I can't go anywhere in town without people stopping me to say how sorry they are about the fire, and wanting to know exactly what happened. I appreciate their concern, but it's wearing me out, not to mention the strain of reliving everything over and over again."

"Staying in sounds good." He followed her into the house, and through to a sunny breakfast room.

"Mrs. Milligan was happy to let me use her kitchen." The table was set for two, with salads and bread already in place, and a bottle of wine chilling in a silver tub. He sat where she directed and a feeling of contentment washed over him—surprising, since he had never considered himself the domestic sort.

While they ate, she talked about her day—the telephone conversations with her guests and the insurance company, and her visit with Brenda. "Do you think Henry Hake could have stumbled upon that old lab and contracted tularemia that way?" she asked.

"It's possible, I suppose," Rob said. "Though no one has found anything to indicate that. Apparently, tularemia lives in the soil in a lot of areas—so it might have been something as simple as digging a hole and breathing in particles of dirt, and being particularly vulnerable because of his heart condition."

"It probably is something like that," she said. She refilled their wineglasses. "Oh, I almost forgot—Bryce Reed called me this afternoon and invited me to a press conference he's giving up at Dakota Ridge tomorrow, to publicly unveil CNG's plans for the research facility."

"Still trying to get your support for the project?" Rob asked.

"I suppose. I want to go to the press conference, if only to get another look at the property."

"I'll go with you. I'd like to have another look at it, too," he added, before she could protest that she didn't need a bodyguard.

"I did some digging into Bryce Reed's background today," he said.

"Oh?" Paige laid down her fork and gave him her full attention. "What did you find out?"

"He's been chief financial officer for CNG for nine months, in charge of special projects. Apparently this research lab is a special project. Before that, he worked for a couple of oil companies, a financial management firm and a manufacturing conglomerate. Pretty run-of-the-mill corporate stuff."

"So nothing juicy?" Paige picked up her fork again and resumed eating the lasagna she had prepared.

"Not in his business life. His personal life is a little more interesting."

Her mouth full, she nodded that he should continue.

"He's been married three times, divorced three times. Five children, none of whom live with him."

"None of that makes him a bad person," Paige said. "I'm divorced."

"I never said it did. No, the interesting part is how he spends his time outside of work. He's been a member of several organizations the FBI classifies as fringe groups."

Paige wrinkled her nose. "What does that mean? I imagine more than a few people here in town consider Eagle Mountain environmentalists to be a fringe group."

"In this case, these are extremist groups that have advocated for things like white supremacy and limiting voting in elections to those with a certain income level."

"Is he a member of any of those groups now?" she asked.

"No. And he's never been convicted of a crime."

"So maybe those earlier affiliations were mistakes of his youth and he's a more moderate thinker now." She pushed her plate away and sipped her wine. "Lots of people make mistakes when they're young. They shouldn't have to pay for them the rest of their lives."

Rob was sure she was thinking of Parker. "Your brother came to see me this morning," he said.

She straightened. "He didn't come to see me. I haven't even talked to him since yesterday."

"He volunteered to help in any way he could to find out who has been harassing you."

Her expression softened. "And he accuses me of worrying too much about him. What did you tell him?"

"I don't know that there's much he can do—not now, at least." He decided not to mention Parker's story about the helicopter and the men with guns. She was worried enough without that burden. "I'm not even sure where to focus our efforts. I can't figure out if CNG is legit or not—they're deliberately calling attention to themselves with this new high-altitude research facility, when they could have pretended they weren't going to do anything at all with the land, and probably gotten away with whatever they wanted for a long time. So maybe they really have nothing to do with any criminal activity and someone has simply been using land they thought was vacant. Something else interesting I found out about them."

"What's that?"

"Your mayor, Larry Rowe, is a stockholder in CNG."

"You're kidding." She paused, thinking. "That's a conflict of interest, isn't it?"

"It could be. Especially if he received the stock recently, in exchange for his support for the Dakota Ridge project. I haven't had time to dig into that yet."

"I always suspected Larry was for sale to the highest bidder," Paige said.

"Reed is the man I'm most interested in," Rob said. "I asked my admin to do some more digging."

"I think we should get to the site early tomorrow," Paige said. "I want to hike up the trail and see if he kept his promise to take down the gate over the trail."

"And if he hasn't?"

"If he hasn't, I might have to raise the question at his press conference."

"That won't make him happy."

"I'm not interested in making him happy," she said. "I'm interested in making things right."

That was the Paige Rob knew best—the crusader, ready to wage battle and defeat injustice. She ignored her vulnerability by being strong. How could he get past the toughness she wore like body armor and prove she had no need for shields with him?

Chapter Fourteen

Paige couldn't have asked for a better day for a hike when she and Rob set out on the Dakota Ridge Trail the next morning before CNG's press conference. The autumn air was so crisp it practically crackled, and the gold of aspen leaves carpeted the trails and shone bright against a Colorado blue sky. Eyes closed, she breathed in deeply of the pine-scented air, her muscles unknotting as some of her tension eased.

"It's better than a tranquilizer, isn't it?" Rob asked. He had pulled a day pack from the back seat of her car and shrugged into it. Dressed in hiking boots, jeans and a flannel shirt worn open over a black T, he didn't look like a cop today—if you ignored the pistol under that shirt, which she intended to do.

"I need the outdoors like some people need coffee," she said. She wore her own pack over a cropped denim jacket, skinny jeans and a muted gold turtleneck. "And this is one of my favorite places—which is why I was so upset when the gate was installed over the trail." She led the way up the red dirt path.

Rob fell into step beside her. "I did a lot more of this kind of thing before I moved to Denver," he said. "I used to hike in the Alleghenies almost every weekend when I lived in West Virginia."

"Why did you stop?" she asked. "It's not like Denver doesn't have hiking trails."

He shrugged. "I got busy at work. I didn't have anyone to go with. Really, I think I just got lazy. You've reminded me of what I've been missing." His eyes met hers and she wondered if he meant he had been missing more than hiking.

She looked away and he continued, "I'm still hoping to get in some fishing before I leave town."

She didn't look at him. "And when will that be?"

"The fishing? I don't know. It depends on the case."

"I meant, when will you be leaving town?"

"That depends on the case, too."

Right. But he *would* be leaving. She needed to remember that.

He took her hand in his. "I'm not going yet," he said. "Maybe I'll take you with me fishing."

Her breath had stopped at the words *maybe I'll take you with me*, and then she scolded herself for being so foolish. Since when had she wanted a man to take her anywhere? To his bed, maybe. Out to dinner occasionally. She appreciated a man who took her into his confidence, though she could admit she didn't readily return the favor. No, she didn't want

Rob to take her anywhere. She didn't know what she wanted from him, really, and the idea frustrated her. She was never this indecisive about anything. Could she blame the stress she was under, with the threats on her life and the destruction of her home and livelihood?

Beside her, Rob tensed, one hand reaching for the gun beneath his shirt, the other at her back. "What is it?" she asked, fear tightening her throat and making the words come out strained.

"I thought I heard someone over there." He nodded toward the fence that marked the boundary of CNG's property.

They stood still, listening. After a long moment, Paige shook her head. "I didn't hear anything. It was probably just a bird or a deer or something."

"You're right." He took his hand from the gun, but kept his palm against her back. "As beautiful as it is up here, it spooks me."

"Me, too. And that makes me even angrier. Whoever fired those shots took away my peace of mind in the wilderness."

"The way to regain that peace is to fight back," he said.

"Yes. And that's exactly what I intend to do." She quickened her pace as they passed the place where the shots had been fired, but she couldn't resist the urge to look in that direction. There was nothing to see but an opening in the trees and part of the fence.

Rob put a hand on her back again. He didn't say anything, but he didn't have to. The warm, firm weight of his touch told her he had faith in her to fight through this—and that he would be fighting with her. "I should have brought the bolt cutters and hacksaw with me," she said, her tone teasing. "Would you have to arrest me if I cut off the lock?"

"I don't know," he said. "I might have to place you in my personal custody."

"You might have to handcuff me to keep me from escaping."

"I might have to," he said. "And do a thorough search to make sure you aren't carrying any weapons."

The slope they were climbing had little to do with her heavy breathing now. She hoped the press conference was short. She would suggest they go back to Rob's hotel room and try out some of his ideas.

He must have had the same idea, because he began to walk faster, and she hurried to keep up. They topped a rise and she could see the gate—and the section of trail where the gate wasn't supposed to be. The heavy iron structure was still in place, blocking the way, with heavy barbed wire preventing anyone from getting around it.

She stopped and swore.

"When did Reed say he was going to remove it?" Rob asked.

"Right away, I thought," she said. "Just wait until I see him. I'm going to give him a piece of my mind about this. And I'll make sure every reporter at this press conference hears. If he expects my support for this project, then he needs to keep his promises. He can't restrict public access to a historic trail. This hiking trail has been in use for over a hundred years. The easement transfers with the title and all his money and power can't make it go away. When I finish with him—"

She stopped, aware of Rob's calm gaze on her. He looked as if he was trying very hard not to smile. "What?" she demanded. "What's so funny?"

He shook his head. "Nothing's funny. I just love how you're so passionate."

Warmth spread through her body as she remembered how he had brought out another kind of passion in her—one she had kept in check for too many years. Had he deliberately chosen that word to distract her? "At least you didn't tell me I'm cute when I'm angry," she said.

"No, not cute," he said. "Beautiful, and more than a little intimidating—but not 'cute.'"

He shuddered, and she couldn't help but laugh. She took his hand. "Come on. Let's get over to the press conference."

On the way back down the trail, she stopped again at the opening where she had looked in and seen the two men with the crate. "While I'm holding Reed's feet to the fire," she said, "I'm going to ask him to walk back here with me and look for that opening where the two men I saw stowed the crate. He says he has nothing to hide—let him prove it."

"He's not going to know what hit him," Rob said.

"By the time I'm done," she said. "I have a feeling Bryce Reed is going to wish he hadn't invited me today."

They returned to the car and, after she unlocked it, stashed their packs in the back once more. Instead of then going to the passenger door, however, Rob took a slow walk around the vehicle, studying it carefully.

"What are you doing?" she asked.

"Making sure no one's tampered with it while we were gone." His eyes met hers over the top of the car, and his grave expression sent a shiver down her spine. "Just being careful."

"Do you see anything?" she asked.

He opened the passenger door. "No. I think we're fine."

Her heart sped up when she turned the key in the ignition, movie scenes of exploding cars replaying in her brain. But the engine turned over smoothly and she backed out of the parking space without incident.

The gates to the resort compound were open. The first thing she noticed was that the fading sign advertising the resort had been replaced with a new placard that proclaimed this was the Future Home of Dakota Ridge Research and Development, a project of CNG Development.

The second thing she noticed was that hers was the only car in sight. "Where is everybody?" she asked. She checked the time. Nine forty-five. "The press conference is supposed to start at ten. I would think at least some people would be here by now. Reed, at least, should be here."

"Let's take a look around," Rob said. "But do me a favor and drive back out and park on the shoulder of the road."

"Why?" she asked, even as she turned the car around.

"If someone comes along and closes that gate, you don't want to be stuck in here."

She stared at him. "Do you always think in terms of worst-case scenarios?"

"It's part of my training."

She parked on the shoulder, facing toward town, and they both got out and walked back up to CNG's property, and through the open gates. Their footsteps sounded overly loud on the gravel, and louder still as they crunched over a carpet of dried leaves that had settled in a low spot where the asphalt had worn away from what had once been the main street of the resort.

She zipped up her jacket and fought off a chill. "Maybe I got the time wrong," she said. "Maybe it's supposed to be at noon instead of ten. Though I could have sworn Reed said ten."

"The gate's open," Rob said. "Someone's been up here."

"Then where are they now?" She stopped and scanned the empty streets and abandoned buildings. Empty landscapes usually didn't upset her. Deserted forests and vacant mountaintops usually made her feel surrounded by peace. But this ghost town, where people had tried and failed to make their mark, creeped her out right down to her toes.

Rob took her arm, breaking the eerie spell. "Come on," he said. "Let's go find out where everyone is."

"THIS PRESS CONFERENCE will be the perfect opportunity for us to visit CNG's Dakota Ridge property with no worries about trespassing." Professor Gibson wore an excited expression that made him look years younger than the eightysomething he would admit to. "As much as I appreciate you doing the legwork so far, I'm determined to see the place for myself."

"I doubt they're going to let people wander anywhere they please," Parker said. "And maybe they're only going to let in people they've invited. Paige said Bryce Reed from CNG called to invite her."

"My guess is there will be a lot of people there," the professor said. "You can't keep something like this quiet in a small town. Everyone in the county who can make the time will be there to see what's so special it has to be protected with a big iron gate and razor wire. They won't be able to keep track of all of us. Besides, I intend to question this CNG executive— Reed—to try to determine how much he knows about local history. It could be his bunch has already located the secret lab and is keeping the find to themselves."

"If they're doing that, they won't tell you about it," Parker said.

"You might be surprised how persuasive I can be in my 'teacher' guise," Gibson said. "Most people are conditioned from a young age to obey that voice of authority. It's a very hard habit to break."

Parker wasn't buying it, but he kept quiet about

it. The professor did have an uncanny way of getting things done. "Paige said the press conference is at ten," he said. "What time do you want to leave?"

"I want to get there a few minutes early," Gibson said. "I can introduce myself to Mr. Reed and talk to him while you have a look around. You still have the map I gave you?"

"Yes, sir." Parker grinned. He might have guessed the old man intended for him to do his dirty work. Which was fine by Parker. Working with the professor was way more exciting than delivering pizza or writing English papers.

"We'll take my car." Gibson handed Parker the keys to the late-model Nissan. "You drive. And park on the road—not on the property itself. I would rather walk than get caught in the press of people leaving."

"Okay." Parking on the road was better if they needed to make a quick getaway, too.

"I've uncovered some new material on how Russia tested tularemia as a weapon of mass destruction in some very remote populations on the steppes," Gibson said. "Fascinating stuff."

For the rest of the drive out of town and up toward Dakota Ridge, the professor retold the tales of Russian experimentation, which were both fascinating and horrifying.

"The US didn't do anything like that, did they?" Parker asked.

"Not that I have been able to determine," Gibson said. "Of course, the work they were doing in Ray-

ford County lasted less than a decade. I think by the
end, they had determined that tularemia wasn't as
effective a method of infecting a large number of
people as things like anthrax or Q fever."

"Not with the antibiotics we have today, right?"
Parker asked.

"Antibiotics don't do any good if you don't ad-
minister them," Gibson said. "In remote areas, or
on particularly vulnerable populations, I imagine it
would still be quite harmful."

They fell silent for the rest of the drive, Parker remembering the last time he had been up here—the
day he had watched a helicopter land and a mysterious tall man in a suit and two men in camo emerge.
He hadn't told the professor about that yet. Partly because he didn't want to upset the old man, and partly
because he worried Gibson would call off the search
for the lab just when they were so close to finding it.

"I had expected more traffic coming up here,"
Gibson said, as they passed the turnout for the hiking trail and climbed toward the entrance to CNG's
property. "Park anywhere in here." He motioned to
the side of the road.

Parker swung the car around so that it faced back
toward town, and parked on the shoulder. He got
out and waited while the professor unfolded himself
from the seat and stood. Then he locked the vehicle
and pocketed the keys. He figured he would be driving back, so he might as well keep them.

They walked up the road a short distance and
turned in at the entrance to the property. The profes-

sor stopped first, staring at the big iron gate, which was pulled over the drive and locked with a large padlock. Parker stared at the lock, then shifted his eyes to a piece of paper affixed to the gate with duct tape.

The professor moved toward the paper, and Parker followed. The note, written on what looked like a plain 8½-by-11-inch piece of copy paper, was neatly typed, and read, "Today's press conference has been canceled. It will be rescheduled for a later date. We apologize for the inconvenience."

That was it—no explanation and no signature. The professor pushed back the sleeve of his jacket and checked his watch—a big, old-fashioned nickel-colored one with an expandable metal band. "It is almost exactly ten o'clock," he said.

"There must have been other people who didn't get word about the cancellation," Parker said. "Where are they?"

"I don't know." The professor tugged at the gate. It didn't move. He looked at the fence on either side, which had wicked curls of razor wire along the top. *Prison wire*, Parker thought, then pushed the thought aside.

"Did you say there's another way in?" the professor asked.

"There is, but you have to climb a tree. It's pretty rough going."

Gibson took Parker's arm. "Show me. And don't look at me as if I've lost what mind I have left. I was quite the athlete in my day. I think I can handle a tree. And I didn't come this far not to get a look at this place."

Chapter Fifteen

"I feel like an extra in some B-grade horror movie," Rob said, as he and Paige made their way down the deserted streets. He stared hard at the few remaining buildings. "I keep expecting a badly made-up zombie to lurch out at us."

"You're not helping," she said, and took his arm. "Maybe we should leave. Obviously, no one is here."

"Someone is here," Rob said.

"What makes you say that?"

He shrugged. "It's like when you're in a room in the dark—you can tell someone else is there because the air is different."

She looked at him as if he had grown an extra head. "I have no idea what you're talking about."

"Maybe it's a cop thing."

"Or maybe you're paranoid."

"Maybe that, too."

She inhaled slowly and straightened her shoulders. "If someone else is here, that means they're watching us," she said. "So I really think we should leave."

"We'll leave in a little bit," he said. "But something is going on here, and I'd like to find out what."

She nodded. "Yeah. I would, too. But I'd like to do it without getting shot at this time."

"Me, too." He took her arm and pulled her closer. "We'll just look around a little more. If we don't find anything, we'll leave. Why don't we try to find that entrance you saw to that underground chamber?"

This idea apparently intrigued her enough to set aside her fear. "It's nearer the fence," she said. "Do you remember where I showed you?"

"I think so." He led the way across a crumbling foundation, rusting rebar jutting up from the concrete, weeds sprouting in cracks. They both jumped when a chipmunk darted in front of them.

Paige gave a nervous laugh. "Maybe that was a zombie squirrel," she said.

"Can't be," Rob said. "He wasn't badly dressed."

They relaxed a little after that. Moving into the woods, out of the open, helped, he thought. He didn't feel so exposed in the shelter of the trees. They moved slowly, studying the ground for any sign of a trapdoor or grate, or any access to an underground chamber.

"I know I didn't imagine those two men disappearing into the ground with that crate," Paige said, frustration tightening her voice. "I'm sure it was right around here. I can see the fence where I was standing." She gestured toward the iron bars, and the small opening in the trees on the other side.

"They would have hidden it well," Rob said. "Let's keep looking."

He moved forward a few more steps, scanning the ground. Behind him, Paige let out a cry. "Rob. Come here!"

When he joined her, she was kneeling in the dirt and leaves, tugging at what he thought at first was a tree root. "I think this is the handle to the trapdoor," she said. "I remember now one of the men lifted a door out of the way before he climbed down into the hole."

Rob dropped to his knees beside her and together they raked back dirt and leaves to reveal a square piece of rusty steel, with a metal handle attached. He stood and helped Paige to her feet, then took hold of the handle and tugged. "Uh." He let out a grunt. "It's heavy."

"Let me help." She wedged her fingers next to his and together they hauled back on the door. With a groan of metal on metal, it shifted, and they managed to drag it aside.

They leaned over and stared down into a black opening. Cool air hit Rob in the face, bringing the scents of damp earth and rusting metal. He pulled his phone from his pocket and switched on the flashlight app, then shone the beam into the opening, illuminating an iron-runged ladder affixed to wooden timbers sunk into the earth. But the darkness beyond quickly swallowed up the light.

"I think it might be an old mine shaft," he said.

"Just down in the ground like this?" she asked.

"Don't they usually have some kind of structure over them?"

"Maybe there was one, but it was torn down," he said. "Or the main entrance is somewhere else and this is just a side tunnel someone decided to access. The ladder looks new." He leaned over, trying to see into the darkness. "I wonder what's down there."

Paige took a step back. "I'm not going to go check."

"No." He pocketed the phone again. "Maybe we can get a warrant and come out here with a team." Someone had gone to a lot of trouble to conceal this place, and he wanted to know why. And he wanted to find out what those two men had been hiding down there that had been so important they had tried more than once to kill Paige. "I'd like—"

But he never finished his sentence, as the rapid tattoo of gunfire echoed off the ridge. Men's voices shouted, and branches popped and the ground rumbled with the pounding of running feet.

"We have to get out of here before they see us," Paige said.

But it was already too late for that. A man in forest camo emerged from the woods and raised a rifle to his shoulder. Rob shoved Paige hard toward the opening in the ground. "Get down there," he said.

He was prepared to force her out of the range of gunfire if he had to, but she didn't argue, merely descended the ladder. Rob dropped in after her, as bullets struck the dirt near his head. At the last minute, he reached up and, strengthened by fear and dire need, dragged the trapdoor back into place.

"What do we do now?" Paige's voice trembled as it came to him in the utter darkness.

Rob switched on his flashlight again to illuminate a narrow tunnel lined with rock and timbers. He took Paige's cold hand in his. "Now we run."

THE PROFESSOR NAVIGATED the fallen tree with more agility than Parker would have expected. The old man seemed energized by this adventure, striding through the woods ahead of Parker, looking around with interest. "Do you have the map?" he asked, when they were several hundred yards into the property.

"Right here." Parker took the map the professor had drawn and unfolded it.

Gibson studied the drawing, one hand rubbing his chin. "I think we're about here," he said, pointing to a spot on the map. "So we want to walk this direction." He indicated a large circle on the map. "I think the lab we're looking for is somewhere within this perimeter."

"That's a pretty big area," Parker said. Judging by the scale of the map, the circle took in half a dozen acres or more.

"Then we'd better get busy." The professor pocketed the map. "We have a lot of ground to cover."

They started walking again, but hadn't gone far when a volley of gunfire froze them in their tracks. "We'd better get out of here," Parker said, and turned to leave.

The professor grabbed his arm. "We need to see what—or who—they're shooting at."

Parker gaped at him. "Why do we need to see that? And what makes you think they won't decide to start shooting at us?"

"Come on." The old man pulled on his arm, a lot harder than Parker would have thought possible. "We won't let them see us. But we need to find out what's going on so we can report it to the sheriff."

Reluctantly, Parker let the professor lead him in the direction of the shots. After all, he couldn't run off and abandon the old guy. And despite his heart beating so hard his chest hurt, he had to admit he was curious.

They crept through the trees, keeping to the deepest shadows and moving as soundlessly as possible. They both froze when a man in forest camo ran past, cradling a rifle to his chest. He was only about five feet from them, but he never saw them, so intent was he on his destination somewhere ahead.

They stood frozen for several minutes, Parker scarcely daring to breathe. The professor's fingers dug into his arm, but Parker didn't flinch. "We need to leave," he whispered, trying again.

"Not yet," Gibson said, and started forward, in the direction the man with the gun had run.

Parker wanted to tell the old fool that while he might have lived a full life and not care if he lost it now, Parker had a lot of good years left, and he wanted to enjoy them all. But then he remembered the professor's tales of growing up in the Great Depression and fighting in Korea, and knew the man wasn't foolhardy; he was just a lot tougher than Parker would ever be. And Parker couldn't let him walk into whatever trouble was up ahead alone. So he tried to straighten his shoulders and not think about getting killed, and walked on.

The gunshots grew louder and more frequent. The two of them reached the edge of a clearing and Parker had to bite his lip to keep from crying out. Ahead of them, Paige and Rob crouched on the ground as half a dozen men with guns ran toward them. Parker closed his eyes, not wanting to see his sister cut to pieces by bullets. Then he opened them again, unable to abandon her to her fate.

"We have to do something!" he whispered to the professor.

Gibson remained silent, though his grip on Parker tightened, as if he feared the younger man might charge into the clearing.

As they stared, Paige and Rob disappeared. Or rather, they dropped out of sight, apparently into a hole in the ground. Rob pulled some kind of trapdoor after them.

Parker's eyes met the professor's, who had pulled out his cell phone and was taking photographs—though his hand shook so badly, Parker wondered how in-focus those pictures would be. He took the phone and snapped a few more shots of the scene, amazed that his own hand was so steady. Then he passed the phone back to the professor, who pushed it into his pocket and motioned that they should head back the way they had come.

Parker glanced over his shoulder at the men with guns standing around the now-closed trapdoor. He hoped he and the professor could get help in time. Or that hole in the ground might as well be Paige's grave.

Chapter Sixteen

Paige followed Rob down the long, dark corridor. Or rather, she followed the glow of his cell phone, which reflected dirt walls braced with rocks and timbers slick with moisture. The floor they ran on was wet, too, so they occasionally slipped and caught themselves by grabbing hold of the wall. "Where are we going?" she said to Rob's back.

He stopped, one hand braced on a timber, and looked back at her. "I don't know," he said. "But the farther away we get from that trapdoor, the better."

"They know where we are," she said. "They don't have to hurry." Whoever "they" were.

He raised his hand. "Listen."

She held her breath and focused on detecting any sound. Was that the scrape of metal on metal as they opened the trapdoor—or merely her own ragged breathing?

Rob frowned. "They're not coming in after us," he said.

"Like I said, they don't have to hurry. Maybe they're waiting for more men to show up, with more guns." She shuddered, picturing the figures in military fatigues who had run out of the woods, guns blazing. The shock had been like stumbling onto a battlefield in the middle of an otherwise peaceful setting.

"Why wouldn't they come after us?" Rob asked. "They saw us climb down here."

Times like this, she wished her imagination wasn't quite so vivid. Maybe their pursuers hadn't followed them down here because they were going to flood the tunnel with gas and asphyxiate them. Maybe they'd throw explosives in after them. Maybe they intended to just seal them off and let them starve to death down here. She didn't say any of this—saying the words out loud would make them too real.

She swallowed hard, forcing back panic. "Why do you think they didn't come after us?" she asked.

He looked up and down the corridor. "I think there's another entrance," he said. "Maybe one that's easier to access." His eyes met hers, difficult to read in the dim light. "But they'll have someone—probably a couple of people—watching the trapdoor, to make sure we don't get out that way."

Paige felt light-headed and weak in the knees. She steadied herself with one hand on the clammy stone wall. "You mean we're trapped down here?"

"Maybe not," he said. "Maybe there's another way out."

"A way they don't know about?" That didn't seem likely.

He touched her arm. "Let's keep moving."

She looked around at the narrow, dark passage and tried not to think about the tons of rock over their heads, or the creepy crawlies that might lurk in the darkness. "What are we going to do?" she asked.

"Come on. Let's go."

They started forward again, walking instead of running this time. "Do you think Bryce Reed is behind all this?" Paige asked. Maybe she shouldn't talk, and instead try to move as silently as possible, but what was the point? Their pursuers knew they were down here, and so far this narrow tunnel was the only place they could be. And talking—thinking out loud about what had happened and giving her mind something to focus on besides their dire circumstances— helped her stay calm. "Was the press conference just a ploy to get me up here?"

"He has to know at least some of what's going on," Rob said. "I've never believed CNG wasn't involved somehow. But why try to lure you up here? Most likely you would have seen no one was here, turned around and gone home. I was the one who suggested staying to look around."

"And I went along with you—willingly. I'm not going to play the guilt game."

He looked at her so long without saying anything that she began to feel uneasy. "What?" she asked. "Why are you looking at me like that?"

"You're incredible, did you know that?"

You're incredible, too. But she bit back the words. They sounded so sappy, and not nearly adequate to convey all she was feeling right now. She had started out hating this man, because of what she thought he had done to her brother, and for what she thought he represented. He knew how she felt, and yet he had come through for her at every turn. "Incredible" didn't begin to express what she was feeling, and part of her—she could admit this, if only to herself— part of her was waiting for him to fail her. For him to show another, uglier side, the way her ex-husband had. The way most people had.

"Come on," she said. "I want to hurry and get out of here."

They had traveled perhaps another hundred yards when the tunnel began to widen slightly, until they were able to walk side by side. Light glowed up ahead. "Is that an exit?" she asked, and began to walk faster.

He took her arm, forcing her to slow down. "Careful," he said, and drew his gun from its holster.

She moved in behind him and let him go first. They hadn't gone much farther before she realized the light they were seeing wasn't from outside the tunnel, but the glow of electric lights. They came to an intersection. The main tunnel continued straight into darkness, while a shorter side turning led to the source of the illumination—a room whose door stood open.

"Wait here," Rob whispered, motioning for her to stand in the main tunnel, just out of sight.

She wanted to protest, to insist that she go with him. But what could she do if they ran into trouble? She didn't have a weapon. At least if she stayed here she could try to go for help if he ran into trouble. She pressed her back against the rough stone of the tunnel wall and waited, counting the seconds. "One Mississippi, two Mississippi…"

She was at fifty Mississippi when Rob called to her. "It's all right. Come look at this."

Still uneasy, she walked down the short hallway and stood in the open doorway, and gasped when she saw the concrete-floored, brightly lit chamber. Rob stood in the middle of the high-ceilinged room, next to a stainless-steel counter lined with lab equipment. Paige recognized a microscope, Bunsen burner, racks of test tubes, beakers and various glass flasks. Several crates were stacked against the wall, like the one she had seen being carried down here. There were many more items she couldn't identify, all of which looked technical and complicated. "It's a laboratory," she said.

"Yes," Rob said. He picked up a flask half filled with a dark liquid and squinted at it. "And unlike the last one we found, this one is clearly in operation." He set the flask down.

She joined him in front of the workbench. "This doesn't look like World War II–era equipment," she said. "What are they doing down here? And who is doing it? Reed didn't strike me as the scientific type."

"I don't know who." Rob looked around them. "As for what, I think it might be related to that World

War II operation. Maybe this is the location of that original lab and whoever is behind this decided to update it for their own purposes."

"What purposes?" she asked.

"Henry Hake died of tularemia," he said. "That's one of the diseases the government was supposedly experimenting with back then. What if someone decided to continue that research? Maybe Henry stumbled on it and contracted the disease accidentally—or maybe he was deliberately given it."

She shuddered and wrapped her arms around herself. "Maybe we shouldn't be here," she said. "What if we've already been exposed to something horrible?"

"I don't think there's too much chance of that," he said. "They have to keep the contaminants contained, or no one could work down here." He gestured toward a locked refrigeration unit that hummed in the corner. "Anything dangerous is probably in there."

He pulled out his phone and began taking pictures of the room. Too bad there was no cell service here. He could call for help.

Paige shook her head. No sense dwelling on what they couldn't do. She needed to focus on what they could do. "If you're right about the purpose of this lab, then it would explain a lot," she said. "The secrecy, and the armed guards."

"The willingness to kill people to keep the operation secret," he said.

"Do you think CNG's plans to build a high-altitude

research facility is a cover for this underground operation?" she asked.

"It would be a good one," he said. "It would explain any orders for lab equipment, and any traffic in and out of the property."

"Where are the people who work here now?" Paige asked.

"My guess is Reed sent them away until after the press conference. After that, anyone seeing something like a person in a lab coat would think they were part of the new facility. Reed could even explain away the armed guards as necessary because of the sensitive nature of scientific research."

"The mayor is certainly going to be surprised when he learns his pet project is a big lie," she said. "That won't go well for his career. Is it wrong of me to be a little happy about that, at least?"

Rob reached out and pulled her close. "Remind me to never get on your bad side," he said.

"You've already been on my bad side," she said. She rested one hand on his chest, over the reassuring, strong beat of his heart. "Or have you forgotten already?"

He moved her hand to his lips and kissed her fingers. "I loved that you were so fierce. And you were attracted to me even back then, though you wouldn't admit it."

She pulled her hand away and tried to muster a look of outrage, though she was afraid the most she could manage was amusement. "Just like a man—

imagining that every woman he meets is falling all over herself for him."

"But you're not just any woman." He kissed her cheek.

She wanted to turn her head and capture his mouth with her own, to lean into this moment and let desire and affection obliterate the fear and worry. But that wouldn't be smart, and it wouldn't help get them to safety. So instead, she pulled away from him.

"Come on," she said. "Let's go find a way out of here."

Parker drove with his foot to the floor, the engine in the Nissan screaming in protest. Professor Gibson gripped the dash and spoke through gritted teeth. "You're not going to help your sister if we crash before we get to town. If you slow down, I could call for help."

"There's no phone service up here. And we won't crash," Parker said over the screech of brakes, as the car fishtailed around a hairpin curve. Now wasn't the time for caution. Paige and Rob didn't stand a chance if those thugs with guns caught up with them.

The professor's only answer was a sharp intake of breath as the rear wheels of the car skidded on gravel. Five minutes later, they shot out onto the pavement of the highway that led into town. The needle on the speedometer edged up to ninety. Parker wouldn't have believed the little econobox could go that fast. As they entered the town of Eagle Mountain, a cruiser parked on the side of the road hit its lights and siren and swung in a U-turn to follow them. Parker ignored the cop and kept going, skidding to a stop in front of the sheriff's department. He left the engine running and was out of the car before the professor had unfastened the seat belt.

"Parker Riddell, what the—?" The rest of Deputy Dwight Prentice's shouted question was cut off when the door to the sheriff's department closed behind Parker.

Adelaide Kinkaid looked up from behind her desk in the lobby, then stood as Parker trotted past. "Young man, where do you think you're going?"

"I need to see the sheriff," Parker called over his shoulder.

Sheriff Travis Walker stood in the doorway of his office. "Parker? What's going on?"

"Paige and Rob are in big trouble up on Dakota Ridge."

The professor and Dwight had caught up with him, Gibson looking much paler and older than he had up on the ridge. Dwight had him by the arm and led him to a chair in front of Travis's desk. "I clocked him doing ninety as he came into town," Dwight said. "He's lucky a dog or a kid didn't run out in front of him."

"You have to get as many officers as you can up to Dakota Ridge now, before it's too late," Parker said. They had already wasted too much time.

"Calm down and tell me what's going on," Travis said. He sat behind his desk, clearly not in a hurry to go anywhere.

"We might already be too late!" Parker's voice broke on the words, and he closed his eyes, fighting for control.

Travis turned to the older man. "Professor Gibson, what happened?"

"Bryce Reed invited Paige to a press conference up at CNG's Dakota Ridge property," he said. "Agent Allerton insisted on accompanying her. Parker and I decided to go, as well."

"Why did you and Parker decide to attend the press conference?" Travis asked.

"What does that matter?" Parker asked. "The point is, when we got there, there was no press conference. There wasn't anyone there. The place looked deserted."

"We decided to take the opportunity to look around." The professor took up the story again. "As you may know, I have an interest in the World War II–era laboratory that operated somewhere in the county. My research indicated that the lab was probably in an old mine on the property now owned by CNG Development. I wanted to see if my hypothesis was correct."

"Except we heard gunshots, and then a bunch of men wearing camo came running out of the woods," Parker said. "Then we saw Paige and Rob. The men with guns were shooting at them." He swallowed, still unable to believe what he had seen.

Travis looked at the professor again. "He's telling the truth," Gibson said. "Paige and Rob managed to escape by descending into a hole in the ground, and pulled a trapdoor over them." He leaned forward, hands gripping the arms of the chair. "In thinking it over, I believe they may have found an entrance into the mine where that historic lab is probably located. I'm almost sure of it."

"What happened then?" Travis asked.

"What happened is that we got out of there and came to get you," Parker said. "You've got to do something."

Travis nodded. "How many men with guns did you see?" he asked.

"A dozen," Parker said.

"There were six," the professor said. His eyes met Parker's. "It seemed like more, with all the shooting, but I took the time to count. There were six."

"We'll need reinforcements," Travis said. He picked up the phone.

"Who are you calling?" Parker asked.

"We'll need to get the SWAT team from Junction here."

"We don't have time for that," Parker protested.

"We can't go in without a plan and enough personnel to overwhelm them," he said. "If you want us to save your sister, we need a little time to prepare."

"We don't have time," Parker said again, though with less fervor. "They could already be dead."

"I hope not," Travis said. "But going in unprepared won't save them."

"Parker." The professor's voice, strong and steady, cut through some of his panic.

He looked at his mentor. "What?"

"Remember that Paige is with Agent Allerton,"

Professor Gibson said. "He's a trained law enforcement officer, and he's armed. And I believe he will do everything in his power to protect her."

Parker nodded. He wanted to believe that. He couldn't afford not to believe it. "What do we do now?" he asked.

The professor motioned to the chair beside him. "We wait. And we pray."

BEYOND THE LABORATORY, half a dozen smaller tunnels branched off from the main corridor. Paige and Rob shone the light of Rob's phone down some of these. Most of them led nowhere, either blocked by piles of debris and collapsed timbers, or simply unfinished, as if the original miners who had excavated here had found nothing worth further exploration.

"How far have we walked?" Paige asked after a while. Her feet ached from navigating the uneven, rocky tunnel, and the damp chill underground had settled in, so that she shivered every time they stopped to rest or check out a detour.

"A couple of miles, I think," Rob said. "I understand some of these old mines extend for miles."

"I can't believe no one has come after us yet," she said. "Are they going to try to starve us out?"

Rob didn't answer. Instead, he illuminated yet another niche carved out of the rock, this one starting about five feet above the level of the main tunnel. "They didn't get very far with this one," he said. "Or maybe it was supposed to hold some kind of equipment?"

"Unless it leads to a way out of here, I don't care," she said. "Did you hear what I asked? Why hasn't anyone come after us?"

"I heard you, but I don't have an answer." He must be as tired and scared and cold as she was, but he didn't show it. Though maybe what she had mistaken for calm was merely grim determination.

"I wish we'd thought to bring our backpacks from the car," she said. "Then at least we'd have water and food and a warm jacket." The pack she carried hiking was equipped with all kinds of emergency supplies.

"And if I'd brought my submachine gun maybe we could blast our way out of here."

"Do you have a submachine gun?" she asked.

"No. But as long as we're wishing for things, that's what I'd wish for." Rob took her arm and they started forward again, but had gone only a few feet before he yanked her against him, hard. She would have cried out, but he clamped his hand over her mouth. "Listen!" he hissed, so close to her ear she felt the warmth of his breath.

She listened, and heard a sound she thought at first was rain drumming on a metal roof. Her knees turned to jelly as she realized she was hearing the sound of running feet on stone—running toward them.

"This way." Rob yanked her back the way they had come. When they reached the niche in the side of the tunnel, he boosted her up into it, then crawled up beside her, then switched off his phone, plunging them into darkness.

She clung to him, dizzy with fear and disoriented, afraid if she moved she'd go sliding out of the narrow space. She could fall, and never stop falling into the bottomless blackness.

Rob gripped her just as tightly with one hand. She imagined his other hand held his gun. She wondered how many of their attackers he could kill before he was dead himself. Or maybe they would both be dead before he could fire a single shot. She hoped the end was quick, and then in the same breath, rage rose up at the very idea. She was too young to die! And how cruel that she might do so just when she had found a man she could love again.

She hadn't seen that one coming—falling in love with Rob Allerton, of all men. But here in the darkness, with his arm around her and their lives in danger, all the fears and worries that had kept her from love before seemed beyond petty. Here was a man who respected—even admired—her independence, who laughed at what he called her fierceness and who made her feel more alive than anyone she had ever been with. How cruel to find all that only to lose it.

Faint light glowed in the corridor now, and the sound of tramping feet was much louder—louder even than her pounding heart, which hammered painfully in her chest. Surely they would hear it and discover them in their hiding place.

The light grew brighter, the tramping feet louder. These people weren't even trying for stealth, they were so certain that they would find their prey. "Spread out!" one man commanded. "Search all the corridors. They won't have gone far."

She closed her eyes and rested her head on Rob's shoulder. She didn't feel fierce now—only numb and almost paralyzed with weariness. The running men grew closer, closer, the echoes of boots hitting the hard stone floor bouncing off the walls and filling up the narrow space with sound. She clenched her teeth, dug her fingers into Rob's arm and waited for the end.

Time stopped, and she didn't know how long she waited like that, until Rob shook her shoulder. "They're gone," he whispered.

She opened her eyes to darkness again, and silence. She resisted the urge to shake her head and try to unclog her ears. "They didn't see us?" she whispered.

"They didn't see us." He caressed her cheek, then kissed her, his lips strong and tasting so sweet. She returned the embrace, all the love and fear and despair that warred within her distilled into that desperate, drowning kiss. She wanted to throw her arms around him, to climb into his lap and press her body to his, but their narrow hiding place prevented that. She had to settle for the connection of that kiss, tongues twined and lips melding, a communication that went beyond words.

When they broke the kiss she was left breathless, and it was a moment before she could speak. "Maybe this really isn't the time for this," she said.

"Maybe not." He traced her lips with one finger. "But I can think of worse ways to spend my time."

"Rob, I—"

"Shhh." He pressed his finger to her lips. "We'll talk later. Right now we have to go, before they come back."

He climbed down from the niche, then helped her down, and they hurried away, in the opposite direction from where the armed men had headed. Rob kept the phone off, so they had to navigate in the darkness, but it wasn't as difficult as she would have thought. The tunnel was straight and the walls close enough that she could place a hand on either side to guide her way.

When Rob stopped abruptly, she stumbled into his back. "What is it?" she whispered.

"Another side tunnel." He switched on the cell phone and shone the light to their left, then swore under his breath.

Paige bit back a scream and stared at the body of Bryce Reed, slumped against the wall, his throat cut like an awful red grin.

Chapter Seventeen

Rob switched off the light, but he had seen enough to know that Bryce Reed hadn't been dead very long. The blood that spilled over the front of his shirt still shone wetly, and rigor hadn't yet stiffened the body.

"Does this mean Reed didn't know about what was going on, after all?" Paige asked. "He must have stumbled on the operation, the way we did, and they killed him."

"Maybe," Rob said. "Or maybe he was working with them, but had outlived his usefulness to them."

"When those men don't find us, they'll come back this way to search again," she said.

"Yes." They couldn't afford to stay here. "We know there has to be another entrance, since they came that way," he said.

"They'll have someone guarding it," she said.

"But probably only one or two people," he said. "They can't have had that big of a force. The two men you saw that first day on the trail are dead—probably killed because they had attracted too much attention to the operation. Reed is dead. That leaves whoever is in charge—the man in the suit—and half a dozen guards."

"What man in a suit?" she asked. "I never saw a man in a suit."

"Parker saw him. He was up here one day and a helicopter landed. A man in a suit and two guards in fatigues got out and unloaded a crate, like the one you described."

"He never said anything to me about that."

"He didn't want to worry you."

"But he told you. And you're a cop. He doesn't want to have anything to do with cops."

"Neither did you. I guess people can change their minds." Rob had once thought she was an overly protective, cop-hating crusader who viewed him as the devil incarnate. Now she was the dearest person in the world to him. He took her arm. "It doesn't matter now. We need to get to the entrance before they come back. Once we're there, we'll figure out how to get past whatever guards they've established."

"You make it sound so simple," she said, as they started down the tunnel once more. "I wish I had your confidence."

It was more bravado than confidence, but he'd rather go out charging into daylight than cowering in the darkness.

They moved quickly now, more confident with navigating by feel and instinct. The floor had a steady upward incline, a good indication that they were moving toward the surface.

"Do you feel that?" Paige asked. "It's cooler air. I think we're getting close."

"Not far now," he agreed.

Another fifty yards and he could discern the outline of the timbers that shored up the tunnel. "The light must be coming from the entrance," Rob said. He halted and put a hand out to stop her. "Wait here," he said. "I'm going to check things out."

For once, Paige didn't argue, though she squeezed his hand and held on, so that he had to pull away from her. He drew his gun and moved stealthily forward, ears attuned to any sound. Soon he could make out the entrance, or adit, a wooden structure that jutted out from the rock face of the ridge, heavy beams supporting a metal roof. An exit gate made of thick iron bars stood open.

Rob moved forward, staying close to the wall, as much in shadow as possible. He couldn't hear any voices, or people moving about, but he wouldn't risk his life—and he especially wouldn't risk Paige's—on the chance that their pursuers had been careless enough to leave the entrance unguarded. Most likely, one or two people were out there, their guns trained on the adit, waiting for anyone to emerge.

He moved all the way into the adit, stopping when he bumped up against a stack of crates that lined the wooden wall. The lid was partially off one of the boxes. Rob stared down at sticks of dynamite with long fuses attached. Other boxes contained metal construction fasteners and nails. A few lengths of metal pipe lay alongside. Sacks of concrete mix lined the

opposite wall. It looked like someone planned to expand the operation, perhaps by opening up some of
the sealed-off tunnels, or blasting new ones. They
had better know what they were doing, or they could
bring the whole place down.

Bring the whole place down. This thought echoing
in his head, Rob snatched up a handful of dynamite
sticks and retraced his steps to Paige. "Hold these,"
he said, shoving them at her.

"What?" She stared at the objects in her hands.
"Is this dynamite? As in explosives?"

"Yes. And we're going to use it to get out of here."

"How?"

He took the dynamite sticks from her and began
arranging them at the base of one wall of the tunnel.
"I'm going to set up an explosion to collapse the tunnel here. That will keep the men we saw earlier from
traveling back this way. Any guards out front will
probably come in to investigate—or they'll head to
the other entrance to help their coworkers."

"Or they'll stay put and wait for us to come out,"
she said.

"That's a possibility, too, but I'm betting on them
running in to investigate, in which case I'll be ready
to pick them off." He finished arranging the dynamite and stepped back.

"What makes you think you won't bring a ton of
rock down on us?" she asked.

"Because you're going to be waiting up at the entrance. And I'm going to be standing as far away as
possible when the explosion occurs."

"How are you going to light the fuses?" she asked. "We don't have any matches."

"No, but I have this." He drew his gun. "A bullet striking the dynamite will set it off."

She looked doubtful. "And you know this how?"

"Let's just say my friends and I experimented during a kegger when we were young and stupid."

She laughed—nervous, desperate laughter. "It's a crazy, dangerous idea."

"It is," he agreed. "But I can't think of a better one. Can you?"

"No."

"All right." He took another step back. "You go up to the entrance. There are a lot of boxes and stuff piled against the wall. If you crouch down behind them, anyone running past shouldn't see you. After the explosion, I'll wait here to catch whoever comes in to investigate."

"Okay…" She started to move away, then came back and grabbed his shoulders and pulled him down for a fierce kiss. "I love you," she said. "Remember that."

"I love you, too," he said, but she was already gone, hurrying up the tunnel. He hoped that wouldn't be the last time he would see her. Though he had laid out the plan for her as if it was a sure thing, there were plenty of variables he couldn't account for. If things didn't go their way, they might both be dead in a very short time.

PARKER STOOD IN the parking lot for the hiking trail, hands shoved into the pockets of his jeans, staring down the road as if he could somehow see through the trees to what was going on at the abandoned resort. Almost two hours had passed since he had seen those men go after Paige and Rob. She might very well be dead by now.

"The sheriff is doing everything he can." The professor joined him at the edge of the lot. On the other side of the gravel space, Sheriff Walker and his deputies milled about with half a dozen men and women in black pants and shirts, body armor and helmets.

"What are they waiting on?" Parker asked. "Why are they wasting time standing around?"

A sheriff's department SUV pulled into the lot and Gage climbed out. "I've been trying to locate Bryce Reed," he said. "He's not at his office. He's not answering his phone. None of the news outlets knew anything about a press conference."

"He made it up, to get Paige up here," Parker said. "If something has happened to her and he's still alive—"

"Don't say anything rash." The professor gripped Parker's shoulder. "Wait and see what happens."

All he had been doing was waiting. This was worse than being in prison. At least then he had had an idea of when the waiting would end. And he had known that he deserved to be there, to pay for the crimes he had committed. Paige had never hurt anyone. She didn't deserve to die this way.

The sound of tires on pavement made them all turn, to see a black SUV make a screeching turn into the lot. It came close to hitting some of the SWAT members, who jumped back and glared at the new arrival. The driver's-side door opened and a tall man with a crooked nose and heavy jowls stepped out, his expression thunderous.

"You don't have any business here, Larry," Travis said, walking toward him.

"Who is that?" Parker asked the professor.

"That's the mayor of Eagle Mountain, Larry Rowe," he said.

"What is going on here?" Rowe demanded. "Why are all you people here? What's happened?"

"This isn't your concern, Larry," Travis said. "You need to leave."

Parker stared at the mayor, who looked like a boxer. Where had he seen him before, very recently?

"I won't leave," Rowe said. He turned to one of the SWAT team members. "Is this some kind of training exercise? Do you have CNG's permission to be here?"

"We're not on CNG property," Travis said.

"You're adjacent to it," Rowe said. "What you do here could affect them."

"Go home, Mayor," Travis said. "As I said, this doesn't concern you."

"I won't leave until you answer my questions." Rowe folded his arms across his barrel chest. "Just because you have a gun and a badge doesn't mean you can throw your weight around."

Parker moved closer, to get a better look at the mayor. "You're the man I saw here that day," he said. "The man who was in the helicopter."

The mayor glared at him. "Who are you?"

Parker ignored him and turned to Travis. "He was here, on CNG's property," he said. "He landed in a helicopter, with two men in camo, with guns. Like the men who were after Paige and Rob." Was the sheriff believing any of this? He had such a stone face, Parker couldn't tell.

"I don't know what he's talking about," the mayor said. He glared at Parker. "What were you doing on CNG property? That's trespassing. Sheriff, you need to arrest this man for trespassing."

The sheriff stared at Parker, as if he was considering doing just that. Parker took a step back. He had made a mistake, saying anything.

The leader of the SWAT team joined them. In the black clothes with all the extra elbow, knee and shoulder pads, and the heavy helmet, he looked like something out of a cyborg movie. "We're ready to go," he said.

Travis turned to Parker. "You stay here," he said. "We'll radio when it's safe for you to join us."

Parker nodded. "All right."

A car door slammed and they turned in time to see the mayor, tires squealing, speeding out of the parking area. "Want me to go after him?" Gage asked.

"What was that about a helicopter?" Travis asked.

Parker shook his head. "I'll tell you later. Go help Paige."

Travis turned to the others. "All right," he said. "Let's go."

PAIGE CROUCHED BEHIND the crates piled at the entrance to the mine, trying not to think about the sticks of dynamite she had seen lying in the top box like rows of Christmas crackers, but so much more deadly. She watched the entrance, while her ears strained to hear what was going on behind her, back with Rob.

He had promised to stand well away when he fired into the pile of dynamite, but what if something went wrong? What if some fault in the rock made it come down on his head? What if the explosion brought down only part of the wall and the gunmen were able to get through?

What if? What if? She had to stop thinking about all these questions that couldn't be answered and focus instead on what she could control. When the explosion happened, men were likely to come running through that entrance and she had to be ready.

She thought she was prepared for the explosion, but when it came, the shock threw her forward against the crates, and a wave of dust rolled through the tunnel and over her. Her ears rang from the concussion of the blast, so that she was only dimly aware of a deep rumble and a sound like cracking earth. Then all fell silent, so silent she wondered if she had gone deaf.

The light shifted and she looked up to see the silhouette of a man in the mine entrance, broad shouldered and holding a rifle. She ducked down lower behind the boxes, praying he couldn't see her in the haze of dust.

Then he began running, boots pounding hard against the stone as he raced past her. A few seconds more and a single shot pierced the silence. She held her breath, waiting for more, but all was still. She wanted to call out to Rob, to make sure he was safe and alive, but she knew she couldn't. She didn't know who might be listening.

So she kept silent and waited, as seconds and minutes dragged by. She had no idea how much time had passed when a shadow fell over her and she looked up to see a second man in the doorway. This man was shorter than the first, and not as burly, but he, too, carried an automatic rifle. He took a step toward her, and then another. "Jake?" he called.

Jake didn't answer. The second man shifted his rifle so that it pointed forward, his hand near the trigger guard. Would he see Rob before Rob saw him? Would he kill him?

Without moving, Paige scanned the area around her, searching for a weapon. She needed to stop this guy before he got to Rob. He took another step toward her, and another, moving faster now, his rifle at the ready. When he was even with her hiding place, Paige lunged, grabbing on to his calf just below the knee and yanking with all her might.

He went down like a tree felled in the forest. Before he hit the floor, she stood and brought a length of metal pipe down on his head as hard as she could. When the pipe made contact with his skull it sounded like a melon splitting open, and she dropped the pipe in shock. The man moaned, then didn't make another sound.

Paige hurried down the tunnel and met Rob running toward her. "What happened?" he asked, grabbing hold of her.

"Another man came in and I was afraid he was going to kill you, so I hit him with a pipe. I think I might have killed him."

"Let's get out of here," he said, and pulled her toward the entrance.

They had to step around the man she had hit. He lay very still in a pool of blood. "Don't look," Rob said, and tugged her past him.

After spending so much time in the dark tunnel, Paige found the light outside blinding. She and Rob both put up hands to shield their eyes. She expected to see yet another man there with a gun, but there was no one, and she sagged against Rob with relief. "We did it," she said, the words barely audible. "We did it."

"Let's get out of here," he repeated.

"Oh, I don't think you're going anywhere."

They turned at the words and Paige gasped as she recognized the man who had said them. "Larry?"

"Throw down your weapon, Agent Allerton," Mayor Larry Rowe said.

"Larry, what are you doing here?" Paige asked. And with a gun. Larry had always struck her as the quintessential corporate type, comfortable only behind a desk or in a boardroom. Seeing him here, threatening them, threw her off balance.

"You're the man in charge of this operation, aren't you?" Rob asked.

"The gun, Agent Allerton."

Rob tossed the gun into the dirt. Larry kicked it

aside, sending it skittering into the underbrush, well out of reach.

"I don't understand," Paige said. "What are you doing here? That laboratory we saw—are you really making biological weapons down there?"

"So many questions," Larry said.

"Why not give me the answers?" Paige said. "You're going to kill me anyway." The longer she could keep him talking, the longer they would stay alive. And the longer she and Rob might have to see some way out of this dilemma.

"You always did think you were the cleverest person in the room, didn't you?" Larry's mouth twisted into a sneer. "No one dares cross Paige Riddell, because she has all the answers. And yet you had no idea what was going on up here, right under your nose."

"You found the World War II lab and decided to resume the research that was done here," Rob said. "Some foreign organizations will pay a great deal of money for what you could produce there."

"Very good, Agent Allerton," Larry said.

"Did you kill Henry Hake?" Paige asked.

"Henry was happy to lease the land to us after you stalled his plans for his resort," Larry said. "So you could say that you're the one who set all this in motion."

"Why did you kill him?" she asked.

"He discovered what we were doing and objected, so we had no choice but to eliminate him."

"Henry's bodyguard, Ian Barnes, worked for you,"

Rob said. "Henry told everyone Barnes came to him from one of his business partners—that was you. Barnes murdered Henry's lawyer, Andy Stenson."

"Stenson was the first to figure out what we were doing here, so I asked Ian to get rid of him." He shrugged, as if ordering a murder was no big deal.

"Were Wade Tomlinson and Brock Ryan working for you, too?" Paige asked. "The men who murdered Angela and Greg Hood and kidnapped Deputy Gage Walker and his girlfriend?"

"Tomlinson and Ryan were two of my best allies," Larry said. "But they balked at killing that kid, so they had to go, too."

"Those two men whose bodies we found in that burned-out shed—did they work for you, too?"

"Oh yes." He frowned. "I thought they'd take care of you and you'd be out of my way for good, but no such luck. After that, they weren't any use to me."

"So pretty much everyone who helped you ended up dead," Rob said.

"Not everyone," Larry said. "My brother, Garrett, played the part of a billionaire who wanted to buy that mining book from Brenda Stenson. I didn't want someone else to get their hands on it and figure out where the original laboratory was." He chuckled. "He was the 'top secret agent' who fooled Eddie Carstairs, too. That was a role he really liked." Eddie had threatened Brenda Stenson and destroyed the book about the secret World War II laboratory.

"Where is your brother now?" Paige asked.

"In Connecticut, believe it or not. Acting. I told

him I'd pay him a lot more money than some two-bit dinner theater, but he wasn't interested. Go figure."

"Why did you kill Bryce Reed?" Rob asked.

"He was getting nervous about the project," Larry said. "So few people have the courage of their convictions these days."

"But—" she began.

"Enough!" He jabbed the gun in their direction. "Back into the mine."

Paige darted her eyes to Rob's, hoping to see that he had a plan. But the only emotion she could read on his face was the same desperation she felt.

"Quit stalling!" Larry barked.

She lurched forward, stumbling on a rock near the mine entrance, and fell hard, the rough grit scraping her palms. "Get up!" Larry shouted, and fired into the ground near her head.

Rage filled her. How dare he shoot at her while she was down? She closed her fingers around a handful of grit and rose up on her knees. Larry bent toward her and she hurled the grit into his face. The gun went off again, the bullet thudding into the dirt near her feet.

Rob jumped on Larry's back and forced him to the ground, then struck a savage blow to his hand, sending the gun flying. He was kneeling on Larry's back, forcing his face into the dirt, when half a dozen figures in black pants and bulletproof vests and helmets jogged toward them.

"No!" Paige cried, and lunged toward the discarded gun. She hadn't come this far to go down without a fight.

"Paige, it's all right." One of the men raised the visor of his helmet and she recognized Travis. "Put the gun down," he said gently.

She let the weapon fall and sank to her knees. One of the other officers moved forward and secured the mayor, while another helped Rob to stand.

Rob walked over to her, pulled her to her feet and put his arm around her. "Let's get out of here," he said.

She laid her head on his shoulder. "That's the best idea I've heard all day."

Chapter Eighteen

All Paige wanted was to take a shower, have a good stiff drink, eat a steak and collapse, but first she and Rob had to reassure Parker and Professor Gibson that they really were okay. Then they had to repeat the reassurances for Lacy and Brenda and Adelaide and pretty much everyone else in town.

Then they had to tell their story to the sheriff, and tell it again for their official statement. Repeating the details made the events of the last six hours seem even more surreal. It was like recounting a movie, or a horrible dream. Those things hadn't really happened to her, had they? But she had the bruises and scrapes to prove it, and memories that would haunt her for a long time to come.

"We've contacted the authorities in Connecticut," Travis said. "They'll arrest Garrett Rowe for the part he played in all this and we'll extradite him here."

"I'm amazed that Larry persuaded so many people to work with him," Paige said. "I never thought he was particularly charismatic."

"For some people, money substitutes for personality," Rob said.

"What was in the crate you saw them carrying, that first day when you were on the trail?" Travis asked.

"I have no idea," she said. That was one question she hadn't gotten around to asking Larry.

"My guess is it was lab equipment," Rob said. "It will take weeks—maybe months—to collect and analyze everything in that lab. It's also possible one or more of the crates Paige and Parker saw contained lab cultures or samples of bacteria or germs they wanted to experiment with."

"What are you going to tell your aunt about Henry?" Paige asked Rob, remembering what had brought him back to Eagle Mountain.

"I'll tell her the truth—that he was doing business with some bad people and they killed him. That's all she wanted, to know what really happened."

"It's so sad," Paige said. "What does Larry say about all of this?"

"He isn't talking," Travis said. "But with your testimony and Rob's, and the evidence from the site, I don't think we'll have any problem putting him away for a long time."

"What about the armed guards who tried to kill us?" Paige asked.

"We found one of them dead near the mine entrance, and another one with a pretty severe concussion, but he'll live," Travis said. "We arrested four others as they emerged from the trapdoor at the other end of the mine."

"I can't believe so many people died because of this," Paige said. "Andy Stenson, Brock Ryan and Wade Tomlinson, the Hoods, Henry Hake, Bryce Reed—even those two men who tried to kill me were killed because they drew too much attention to the place."

"There were millions, probably billions, of dollars at stake," Rob said. "That's how much some foreign powers would be willing to pay for biological weapons."

"But weapons like that are illegal," Paige said. "I mean, they're against the Geneva convention."

"Some people don't care."

That idea was too depressing to consider.

"I know you're both exhausted," Travis said. "You can go for now, but we'll have more questions for you later, and you'll probably eventually have to testify in court."

Outside, Parker and the professor waited for them. Parker wrapped Paige in a hug that squeezed the breath out of her. "Don't scare me like that again," he said, his voice husky.

She pulled away and studied him. He had dark circles under his eyes and needed a shave. When had the little boy she had loved for so long grown into such a man? "Thanks for calling in the cavalry," she said.

"I understand you told the sheriff about seeing Larry Rowe in that helicopter that landed on CNG property," Rob said.

"Yeah. He said if I agreed to testify about that, he'd overlook the parole violation for trespassing."

"Excuse me." The professor moved closer. "I understand now isn't a good time, but when you've had a chance to rest, I'd appreciate hearing more about the lab you found. Do you really think it's the space used by the government during World War II?"

"It could be," Rob said. "Larry as much as confirmed it. I think finding it gave him the idea to work on developing biological weapons in the first place."

"Then I definitely want to hear more about it. At your convenience."

"Right now I just want a shower and a drink." Paige looked down at her dirty jeans and scraped hands.

"Sure thing," Parker said. "Where do you want me to take you?"

"I'll take care of her." Rob put his arm around her.

Parker took a step back. "I guess you're in good hands, then." Parker looked at Rob. "But if you do anything to hurt her, you'll have me to answer to."

Rob nodded, his expression solemn. "Understood."

When Parker and the professor were gone, Paige looked up at Rob. "Don't worry about him," she said. "If you do anything to hurt me, you'll have *me* to answer to."

"I'm definitely more frightened of you. But you don't have to worry. I won't hurt you. Ever."

"I believe you." She smiled up at him. "Let's go back to your motel."

They didn't speak even after they were inside Rob's room. He merely drew the drapes and she began to strip off her clothes in the dim light from the bedside lamp. Rob did the same, until they stood facing each other, naked. He smoothed a hand along her shoulder, and his fingers trembled. "If anything had happened to you…" he began.

"Shhh." She silenced him with a kiss. "We're both okay," she said, her lips almost touching his. "We're going to be okay."

He nodded and tried to pull her close, but instead, she took his hand and led him into the bathroom. She turned on the shower, jets all the way up and water steaming hot. Then she stepped in and beckoned for him to follow.

She thought of all the ways water could cleanse, from removing dirt from laundry to the soul cleansing of baptism. As they took turns soaping each other's bodies, she felt the strain and fear of the past days wash away, replaced by an exultant joy that they were here now, alive and able to enjoy each other this way.

The water was still warm when Rob tossed aside the soapy washrag and pulled her closer, full against his naked body, her breasts pressed against the firm wall of his chest, her hips just under his. Salty tears mingled with the shower spray as his lips claimed hers, and when he bent his knees and slid into her she stood on tiptoe to accept him, reveling in the sensation of being united with him, yet so fully herself.

They emerged from the shower replete and renewed and ravenous. The motel didn't offer room service, but Rob ordered a large pizza and promised extra if the delivery driver—not Parker—would stop at the liquor store and purchase a bottle of wine. They ate at the table by the window, sipping wine and feeding each other pizza, half-dressed and unable to stop looking at each other.

They made love again in the bed, burrowed under warm covers, alternately giggling with delight and moaning at the depth of their need. When Paige fell asleep in Rob's arms, she didn't dream of anything.

She woke with gray light showing through the gap in the curtains, and stretched like a cat, more relaxed than she could remember being in years. She rolled over onto her side to watch Rob sleeping. He lay on his back, his hair mussed, the dark shadow of beard along his jaw. She knew how intimidating he could look, how insistent he could be on doing the right, legal thing, upholding the commitment he had made as a law enforcement officer. Where once she had bristled at his unwillingness to see gray instead of black-and-white, now she drew comfort from his steadfastness.

Her chest hurt when she thought of how close she had come to losing him. Loving someone this way was so wonderful and so terrifying.

He looked up at her, his brown eyes clear and calm. "How long have you been watching me?" he asked.

"A while." She smiled.

"What does that smile mean? What are you thinking?"

"I'm thinking that I've lost just about everything, and I'm happier than I've ever been."

He reached for her hand and pulled it to his chest. "Marry me," he said.

She tried to pull her hand away, but he held it fast. "This is your romantic proposal?" she asked. "Naked and in bed?"

"I thought you weren't a traditionalist. Do you want me to get down on my knee? I will."

She wrinkled her nose. "What if I say no?"

"I'll keep asking. Are you going to say no?"

She wanted to laugh—he looked so worried. "No. Yes. I don't know."

He shoved himself into a sitting position, forcing her to sit up also, or risk a pain in her neck from trying to look up at him. "You faced down an armed killer yesterday and defeated him with your bare hands," he said. "After that, how can you be afraid of anything?"

"When you put it like that—yes."

"Yes, what?"

"Yes, I'll marry you."

He crushed her to him and kissed her until she was dizzy. Gently, she pushed away from him. "Where will we live?" she asked.

"Where do you want to live?"

"I don't know. Eagle Mountain feels like home, but your work is in Denver. And maybe a change would be good for me."

"I have a feeling I'm going to be here in Eagle Mountain for a while yet."

"Oh?"

"Somebody has to inventory that lab. That's going to take a while, and I already have experience on the property, so I think there's a good chance I'll get the job."

"So we can live here," she said.

"For a while. And then decide what we want to do. After all, we have the rest of our lives to be together."

"Yes, and I hope that's a very, very long time." She settled against him, her head on his shoulder.

"I hope so, too." He wrapped his arm around her.

"One thing's for sure," she said.

"What's that?"

"I'll never have to worry about being bored with you."

"Not every woman would see that as an advantage," he said.

"As you've pointed out before, I'm not every woman."

"Thank God for that."

"Shut up and kiss me."

"Yes, ma'am." And he did.

* * * * *

Look for more
Eagle Mountain books
from Cindi Myers
coming soon!

You'll find them wherever
Harlequin Intrigue books are sold!

SPECIAL EXCERPT FROM

*When wealthy cattleman Callen Laramie is called
back home to Coldwater, Texas, for a Christmas
wedding, he has no idea just how much his
attendance will matter to his family...and to the
woman who's never been far from his thoughts—
or his heart.*

Read on for a sneak preview of
Lone Star Christmas
by USA TODAY *bestselling author*
Delores Fossen.

CHAPTER ONE

DEAD STUFFED THINGS just didn't scream Christmas wedding invitation for Callen Laramie. Even when the dead stuffed thing—an armadillo named Billy— was draped with gold tinsel, a bridal veil and was holding a bouquet of what appeared to be tiny poinsettias in his little armadillo hands.

Then again, when the bride-to-be, Rosy Muldoon, was a taxidermist, Callen supposed a photo like that hit the more normal range of possibilities for invitation choices.

Well, normal-ish anyway.

No one had ever accused Rosy of being conventional, and even though he hadn't seen her in close to fourteen years, Billy's bridal picture was proof that her nonnormalcy hadn't changed during that time.

Dragging in a long breath that Callen figured he might need, he opened the invitation. What was printed inside wasn't completely unexpected, not really, but he was glad he'd taken that breath. Like most invitations, it meant he'd have to do something, and doing something like this often meant trudging through the past.

Y'all are invited to the wedding of Buck Mc-Call and Rosy Muldoon. Christmas Eve at Noon in the Lightning Bug Inn on Main Street, Coldwater, Texas. Reception to follow.

So, Buck had finally popped the question, and Rosy had accepted. Again, no surprise. Not on the surface anyway, since Buck had started "courting" Rosy several years after both of them had lost their spouses about a decade and a half ago.

But Callen still got a bad feeling about this.

The bad feeling went up a notch when he saw that the printed RSVP at the bottom had been lined through and the words handwritten there. "Please come. Buck needs to see you. Rosy."

Yes, this would require him to do something.

She'd underlined the *please* and the *needs*, and it was just as effective as a heavyweight's punch to Callen's gut. One that knocked him into a time machine and took him back eighteen years. To that time when he'd first laid eyes on Buck and then on Rosy shortly thereafter.

Oh man.

Callen had just turned fourteen, and the raw anger and bad memories had been eating holes in him. Sometimes, they still did. Buck had helped with that. Heck, maybe Rosy had, too, but the four mostly good years he'd spent with Buck couldn't erase the fourteen awful ones that came before them.

He dropped the invitation back on his desk and steeled himself up when he heard the woodpecker taps of high heels coming toward his office. Several taps later, his assistant, Havana Mayfield, stuck her head in the open doorway.

Today, her hair was pumpkin orange with streaks of golden brown, the color of a roasted turkey. Probably to coordinate with Thanksgiving, since it'd been just the day before.

Callen wasn't sure what coordination goal Havana had been going for with the lime-green pants and top or the lipstick-red stilettos, but as he had done with Rosy and just about everyone else from his past, he'd long since given up trying to figure out his assistant's life choices. Havana was an efficient workaholic, like him, which meant he overlooked her wardrobe, her biting sarcasm and the occasional judgmental observations about him—even if they weren't any of her business.

"Your two o'clock is here," Havana said, setting some contracts and more mail in his inbox. Then she promptly took the stack from his outbox. "George Niedermeyer," she added, and bobbled her eyebrows. "He brought his mother with him. She wants to tell you about her granddaughter, the lawyer."

Great.

Callen silently groaned. George was in his sixties and was looking for a good deal on some Angus. Which Callen could and would give him. George's mother, Myrtle, was nearing ninety, and despite her advanced age, she was someone Callen would classify as a woman with too much time on her hands. Myrtle would try to do some matchmaking with her lawyer granddaughter, gossip about things that Callen didn't want to hear and prolong what should be a half-hour meeting into an hour or more.

"Myrtle said you're better looking than a litter of fat spotted pups," Havana added, clearly enjoying this. "That's what you get for being a hotshot cattle broker with a pretty face." She poked her tongue against her cheek. "Women just can't resist you and want to spend time with you. The older ones want to fix you up with their offspring."

"You've had no trouble resisting," he pointed out—though he'd never made a play for her. And wouldn't. Havana and anyone else who worked for him was genderless as far as Callen was concerned.

"Because I know the depths of your cold, cold heart. Plus, you pay me too much to screw this up for sex with a hotshot cattle broker with a pretty face."

Callen didn't even waste a glare on that. The *pretty face* was questionable, but he was indeed a hotshot cattle broker. That wasn't ego. He had the bank account, the inventory and the willing buyers to prove it.

Head 'em up, move 'em out.

Callen had built Laramie Cattle on that motto. That and plenty of ninety-hour workweeks. And since his business wasn't broke, it didn't require fixing. Even if it would mean having to listen to Myrtle for the next hour.

"What the heck is that?" Havana asked, tipping her head to his desk.

Callen followed her gaze to the invitation. "Billy, the Armadillo. Years ago, he was roadkill."

Every part of Havana's face went aghast. "Ewww."

He agreed, even though he would have gone for something more manly sounding, like maybe a grunt. "The bride's a taxidermist," he added. Along with being Buck's housekeeper and cook.

Still in the aghast mode, Havana shifted the files to her left arm so she could pick up the invitation and open it. He pushed away another greasy smear of those old memories while she read it.

"Buck McCall," Havana muttered when she'd finished.

She didn't ask who he was. No need. Havana had sent Buck Christmas gifts during the six years that she'd worked for Callen. Considering those were the only personal gifts he'd ever asked her to buy and send to anyone, she knew who Buck was. Or rather she knew that he was important to Callen.

Of course, that "important" label needed to be judged on a curve because Callen hadn't actually visited Buck or gone back to Coldwater since he'd hightailed it out of there on his eighteenth birthday. Now he was here in Dallas, nearly three hundred miles away, and sometimes it still didn't feel nearly far enough. There were times when the moon would have been too close.

Havana just kept on staring at him, maybe waiting for him to bare his soul or something. He wouldn't. No reason for it, either. Because she was smart and efficient, she had almost certainly done internet searches on Buck. There were plenty of articles about him being a foster father.

Correction: the hotshot of foster fathers.

It wouldn't have taken much for Havana to piece together that Buck had fostered not only Callen but his three brothers, as well. Hell, for that matter Havana could have pieced together the rest, too. The bad stuff that'd happened before Callen and his brothers had gotten to Buck's. Too much for him to stay, though his brothers had had no trouble putting down those proverbial roots in Coldwater.

"Christmas Eve, huh?" Havana questioned. "You've already got plans to go to that ski lodge in Aspen with a couple of your clients. Heck, you scheduled a business meeting for Christmas morning, one that you insisted I attend. Say, is Bah Humbug your middle name?"

"The meeting will finish in plenty of time for you to get in some skiing and spend your Christmas bonus," he grumbled. Then he rethought that. "Do you ski?"

She lifted her shoulder. "No, but there are worse things than sitting around a lodge during the holidays while the interest on my bonus accumulates in my investment account."

Yes, there were worse things. And Callen had some firsthand experience with that.

"Are you actually thinking about going back to Coldwater for this wedding?" Havana pressed.

"No." But he was sure thinking about the wedding itself and that note Rosy had added to the invitation.

Please.

That wasn't a good word to have repeating in his head.

Havana shrugged and dropped the invitation back on his desk. "Want me to send them a wedding gift? Maybe they've registered on the Taxidermists-R-Us site." Her tongue went in her cheek again.

Callen wasted another glare on her and shook his head. "I'll take care of it. I'll send them something."

She staggered back, pressed her folder-filled hand to her chest. "I think the earth just tilted on its axis. Or maybe that was hell freezing over." Havana paused, looked at him. "Is something wrong?" she came out and asked, her tone no longer drenched with sarcasm.

Callen dismissed it by motioning toward the door. "Tell the Niedermeyers that I need a few minutes. I have to do something first."

As expected, that caused Havana to raise an eyebrow again, and before she left, Callen didn't bother to tell her that her concern wasn't warranted. He could clear this up with a phone call and get back to work.

But who should he call?

Buck was out because if there was actually something wrong, then his former foster father would be at the center of it. That *Please come. Buck needs to see you* clued him into that.

He scrolled through his contacts, one by one. He no longer had close friends in Coldwater, but every now and then he ran into someone in his business circles who passed along some of that gossip he didn't want to hear. So the most obvious contacts were his brothers.

Kace, the oldest, was the town's sheriff. Callen dismissed talking to him because the last time they'd spoken—four or five years ago—Kace had tried to lecture Callen about cutting himself off from the family. Damn right, he'd cut himself off, and since he would continue to do that and hated lectures from big brothers, he went to the next one.

Judd. Another big brother who was only a year older than Callen. Judd had been a cop in Austin. Or maybe San Antonio. He was a deputy now in Coldwater, but not once had he ever bitched about Callen leaving the "fold." He kept Judd as a possibility for the call he needed to make and continued down the very short list to consider the rest of his choices.

Nico. The youngest brother, who Callen almost immediately discounted. He was on the rodeo circuit—a bull rider of all things—and was gone a lot. He might not have a clue if something was wrong.

Callen got to Rosy's name next. The only reason she was in his contacts was because Buck had wanted him to have her number in case there was an emergency. A *please* on a wedding invitation probably didn't qualify as one, but since he hated eating up time by waffling, Callen pressed her number. After a couple of rings, he got her voice mail.

"Knock knock," Rosy's perky voice greeted, and she giggled like a loon. "Who's there? Well, obviously not me, and since Billy can't answer the phone, ha ha, you gotta leave me a message. Talk sweet to me, and I'll talk sweet back." More giggling as if it were a fine joke.

Callen didn't leave a message because a) he wanted an answer now and b) he didn't want anyone interrupting his day by calling him back.

He scrolled back through the contacts and pressed Judd's number. Last he'd heard, Judd had moved into the cabin right next to Buck's house, so he would know what was going on.

"Yes, it came from a chicken's butt," Judd growled the moment he answered. "Now, get over it and pick it up."

In the background Callen thought he heard someone make an *ewww* sound eerily similar to the one Havana had made earlier. Since a chicken's butt didn't have anything to do with a phone call or wedding invitation, it made Callen think his brother wasn't talking to him.

"What the heck do you want?" Judd growled that, too, and this time Callen did believe he was on the receiving end of the question.

The bad grouchy attitude didn't bother Callen because he thought it might speed along the conversation. Maybe. Judd didn't like long personal chats, which explained why they rarely talked.

"Can somebody else gather the eggs?" a girl asked. Callen suspected it might be the same one who'd ewww'ed. Her voice was high-pitched and whiny. "These have poop on them."

"This is a working ranch," Judd barked. "There's poop everywhere. If you've got a gripe with your chores, talk to Buck or Rosy."

"They're not here," the whiner whined.

"There's Shelby," Judd countered. "Tell her all about it and quit bellyaching to me."

Just like that, Callen got another ass-first knock back into the time machine. Shelby McCall. Buck's daughter. And the cause of nearly every lustful thought that Callen had had from age fifteen all the way through to age eighteen.

Plenty of ones afterward, too.

Forbidden fruit could do that to a teenager, and as Buck's daughter, Shelby had been as forbidden as it got. Callen remembered that Buck had had plenty of rules, but at the top of the list was one he gave to the boys he fostered. *Touch Shelby, and I'll castrate you.* It had been simple and extremely effective.

"Buck got a new batch of foster kids," Judd went on, and again, Callen thought that part of the conversation was meant for him. "I just finished a double shift, and I'm trying to get inside my house so I can sleep, but I keep getting bothered. What do you want?" he tacked onto that mini-rant.

"I got Buck and Rosy's wedding invitation," Callen threw out there.

"Yeah. Buck popped the question a couple of

weeks ago, and they're throwing together this big wedding deal for Christmas Eve. They're inviting all the kids Buck has ever fostered. All of them," Judd emphasized. "So, no, you're not special and didn't get singled out because you're a stinkin' rich prodigal son. *All of them*," he repeated.

Judd sounded as pleased about that as Callen would have been had he still been living there. He had no idea why someone would want to take that kind of step back into the past. It didn't matter that Buck had been good to them. The only one who had been. It was that being there brought back all the stuff that'd happened before they'd made it to Buck.

"Is Buck okay?" Callen asked.

"Of course he is," Judd snapped. Then he paused. "Why wouldn't he be? Just gather the blasted eggs!" he added onto that after another whiny ewww. "Why wouldn't Buck be okay?"

Callen didn't want to explain the punch-in-the-gut feeling he'd gotten with Rosy's *Please come. Buck needs to see you*, and it turned out that he didn't have to explain it.

"Here's Shelby, thank God," Judd grumbled before Callen had to come up with anything. "She'll answer any questions you have about the wedding. It's Callen," he said to Shelby. "Just leave my phone on the porch when you're done."

"No!" Callen couldn't say it fast enough. "That's all right. I was just—"

"Callen," Shelby greeted.

Apparently, his lustful thoughts weren't a thing

of the past after all. Even though Shelby was definitely a woman now, she could still purr his name.

He got a flash image of her face. Okay, of her body, too. All willowy and soft with that tumble of blond hair and clear green eyes. And her mouth. Oh man. That mouth had always had his number.

"I didn't expect you to be at Judd's," he said, not actually fishing for information. But he was. He was also trying to fight back what appeared to be jealousy. It was something he didn't feel very often.

"Oh, I'm not. I was over here at Dad's, taking care of a few things while he's at an appointment. He got some new foster kids in, and when I heard the discussion about eggs, I came outside. That's when Judd handed me his phone and said I had to talk to you. You got the wedding invitation?" she asked.

"I did." He left it at that, hoping she'd fill in the blanks of the questions he wasn't sure how to ask.

"We couldn't change Rosy's mind about using that picture of Billy in the veil. Trust me, we tried."

Callen found himself smiling. A bad combination when mixed with arousal. Still, he could push it aside, and he did that by glancing around his office. He had every nonsexual thing he wanted here, and if he wanted sex, there were far less complicated ways than going after Shelby. Buck probably still owned at least one good castrating knife.

"I called Rosy, but she didn't answer," Callen explained.

"She's in town but should be back soon. She doesn't answer her phone if she's driving."

Callen couldn't decide if that was a good or bad thing on a personal level for him. If Rosy had answered, then he wouldn't be talking to Shelby right now. He wouldn't feel the need for a cold shower or an explanation.

"Rosy should be back any minute now. You want me to have her call you?" Shelby asked.

"No. I just wanted to tell them best wishes for the wedding. I'll send a gift and a card." And he'd write a personal note to Buck.

"You're not coming?" Shelby said.

Best to do this fast and efficient. "No. I have plans. Business plans. A trip. I'll be out of the state." And he cursed himself for having to justify himself to a woman who could lead to castration.

"Oh."

That was it. Two letters of the alphabet. One word. But it was practically drowning in emotion. Exactly what specific emotion, Callen didn't know, but that gut-punch feeling went at him again hard and fast.

"Shelby?" someone called out. It sounded like the whiny girl. "Never mind. Here comes Miss Rosy."

"I guess it's an important business trip?" Shelby continued, her voice a whisper now.

"Yes, longtime clients. I do this trip with them every year—"

"Callen, you need to come," Shelby interrupted. "Soon," she added. "It's bad news."

* * * * *

Don't miss
Lone Star Christmas *by Delores Fossen,*
available now wherever
HQN Books and ebooks are sold.
www.HQNBooks.com

Copyright © 2018 by Delores Fossen

COMING NEXT MONTH FROM
HARLEQUIN®

INTRIGUE

Available October 16, 2018

#1815 RUGGED DEFENDER
Whitehorse, Montana: The Clementine Sisters • by B.J. Daniels
Cowboy Justin Calhoun is thrilled to see Chloe Clementine, the girl he has always loved, back in Whitehorse, Montana, for the holidays. Can he protect her from the secret Santa who is sending her dangerous gifts?

#1816 THE GIRL WHO WOULDN'T STAY DEAD
by Cassie Miles
When her wealthy ex-husband dies under suspicious circumstances, Emily Benton-Riggs inherits a home in Aspen and several artworks. Now someone is trying to kill her. Will Emily's longtime friend and lawyer, Connor Gallagher, be able to save her from the escalating threats to her life?

#1817 MURDER AND MISTLETOE
Crisis: Cattle Barge • by Barb Han
Rancher Dalton Butler and Detective Leanne West must work together to discover who murdered Leanne's niece and a girl from Dalton's past. As sparks fly between them, Dalton and Leanne will need to find the murderer before he or she chooses another victim...

#1818 DELTA FORCE DEFENDER
Red, White and Built: Pumped Up • by Carol Ericson
When impulsive Delta Force soldier Cam Sutton confronts brainy CIA translator Martha Drake about some mysterious emails, a sinister plot to contain the source of those emails endangers them both.

#1819 HIDE THE CHILD
by Janice Kay Johnson
Psychologist Trina Marr must protect a three-year-old child who is mute after witnessing the murder of her family. After the pair is almost killed, army ranger Gabriel Decker is sent to protect them, but a killer will do anything to stop the only witness to a heinous crime from telling the truth...

#1820 WYOMING COWBOY PROTECTION
Carsons & Delaneys • by Nicole Helm
Addie Foster takes a job as a housekeeper at Noah Carson's ranch to save her baby nephew. However, it's not long before the baby's mob-boss father finds her and begins threatening her. Can Noah protect the woman and child he has come to love?

————————

YOU CAN FIND MORE INFORMATION ON UPCOMING HARLEQUIN® TITLES, FREE EXCERPTS AND MORE AT WWW.HARLEQUIN.COM.

HICNM1018

Get 4 FREE REWARDS!

We'll send you 2 FREE Books plus 2 FREE Mystery Gifts.

SUDDEN SETUP
BARB HAN

DESPERATE STRANGERS
CARLA CASSIDY

Harlequin® Intrigue books feature heroes and heroines that confront and survive danger while finding themselves irresistibly drawn to one another.

FREE
Value Over
$20

YES! Please send me 2 FREE Harlequin® Intrigue novels and my 2 FREE gifts (gifts are worth about $10 retail). After receiving them, if I don't wish to receive any more books, I can return the shipping statement marked "cancel." If I don't cancel, I will receive 6 brand-new novels every month and be billed just $4.99 each for the regular-print edition or $5.74 each for the larger-print edition in the U.S., or $5.74 each for the regular-print edition or $6.49 each for the larger-print edition in Canada. That's a savings of at least 12% off the cover price! It's quite a bargain! Shipping and handling is just 50¢ per book in the U.S. and 75¢ per book in Canada*. I understand that accepting the 2 free books and gifts places me under no obligation to buy anything. I can always return a shipment and cancel at any time. The free books and gifts are mine to keep no matter what I decide.

Choose one: ☐ **Harlequin® Intrigue** Regular-Print (182/382 HDN GMYW) ☐ **Harlequin® Intrigue** Larger-Print (199/399 HDN GMYW)

Name (please print)

Address   Apt. #

City   State/Province   Zip/Postal Code

Mail to the **Reader Service:**
IN U.S.A.: P.O. Box 1341, Buffalo, NY 14240-8531
IN CANADA: P.O. Box 603, Fort Erie, Ontario L2A 5X3

Want to try two free books from another series? Call 1-800-873-8635 or visit www.ReaderService.com.

*Terms and prices subject to change without notice. Prices do not include applicable taxes. Sales tax applicable in N.Y. Canadian residents will be charged applicable taxes. Offer not valid in Quebec. This offer is limited to one order per household. Books received may not be as shown. Not valid for current subscribers to Harlequin Intrigue books. All orders subject to approval. Credit or debit balances in a customer's account(s) may be offset by any other outstanding balance owed by or to the customer. Please allow 4 to 6 weeks for delivery. Offer available while quantities last.

Your Privacy—The Reader Service is committed to protecting your privacy. Our Privacy Policy is available online at www.ReaderService.com or upon request from the Reader Service. We make a portion of our mailing list available to reputable third parties that offer products we believe may interest you. If you prefer that we not exchange your name with third parties, or if you wish to clarify or modify your communication preferences, please visit us at www.ReaderService.com/consumerschoice or write to us at Reader Service Preference Service, P.O. Box 9062, Buffalo, NY 14240-9062. Include your complete name and address.

HI18

SPECIAL EXCERPT FROM

HARLEQUIN®

INTRIGUE

A secret Santa is sending Chloe Clementine increasingly threatening gifts. Can cowboy Justin Calhoun save the girl he has always loved?

Read on for a sneak preview of
Rugged Defender
by New York Times *and* USA TODAY
bestselling author B.J. Daniels.

It all began with a kiss. At least that was the way Chloe Clementine remembered it. A winter kiss, which is nothing like a summer one. The cold, icy air around you. Puffs of white breaths intermingling. Warm lips touching, tingling as they meet for the very first time.

Chloe thought that kiss would be the last thing she remembered before she died of old age. It was the kiss—and the cowboy who'd kissed her—that she'd been dreaming about when her phone rang. Being in Whitehorse had brought it all back after all these years.

She groaned, wanting to keep sleeping so she could stay in that cherished memory longer. Her phone rang again. She swore that if it was one of her sisters calling this early…

"What?" she demanded into the phone without bothering to see who was calling. She was so sure that it would be her youngest sister, Annabelle, the morning person.

"Hello?" The voice was male and familiar. For just a moment she thought she'd conjured up the cowboy from the kiss. "It's Justin."

Justin? She sat straight up in bed. Thoughts zipped past at a hundred miles an hour. How had he gotten her cell phone number? Why was he calling? Was he in Whitehorse?

"Justin," she said, her voice sounding croaky from sleep. She cleared her throat. "I thought it was Annabelle calling. What's up?" She glanced at the clock. *What's up at seven forty-five in the morning?*

"I know it's early but I got your message."

Now she really was confused. "My message?" She had danced with his best friend at the Christmas dance recently, but she hadn't sent Justin a message.

"That you needed to see me? That it was urgent?"

She had no idea what he was talking about. Had her sister Annabelle done this? She couldn't imagine her sister Tessa Jane doing such a thing. But since her sisters had fallen in love they hadn't been themselves.

"I'm sorry, but I didn't send you a message. You're sure it was from me?"

"The person calling just told me that you were in trouble and needed my help. There was loud music in the background as if whoever it was might have called me from a bar."

He didn't think she'd drunk-dialed him, did he? "Sorry, but it wasn't me." She was more sorry than he knew. "And I can't imagine who would have called you on my behalf." Like the devil, she couldn't. It had to be her sister Annabelle.

"Well, I'm glad to hear that you aren't in trouble and urgently need my help," he said, not sounding like that at all.

She closed her eyes, now wishing she'd made something up. What was she thinking? She didn't need to improvise. She was in trouble, though nothing urgent exactly. At least for the moment.

Don't miss
Rugged Defender *by B.J. Daniels,*
available November 2018 wherever
Harlequin® Intrigue *books and ebooks are sold.*

www.Harlequin.com

Copyright © 2018 by Barbara Heinlein

HIEXP1018

Need an adrenaline rush from nail-biting tales
(and irresistible males)?

Check out **Harlequin Intrigue**®
and **Harlequin**® **Romantic Suspense** books!

New books available every month!

CONNECT WITH US AT:

Facebook.com/groups/HarlequinConnection

Facebook.com/HarlequinBooks

Twitter.com/HarlequinBooks

Instagram.com/HarlequinBooks

Pinterest.com/HarlequinBooks

ReaderService.com

HARLEQUIN®

**ROMANCE WHEN
YOU NEED IT**

SGENRE2018

Want to give in to temptation with
steamy tales of irresistible desire?

Check out **Harlequin® Presents®**,
Harlequin® Desire and
Harlequin® Kimani™ Romance books!

New books available every month!

CONNECT WITH US AT:

Facebook.com/groups/HarlequinConnection

Facebook.com/HarlequinBooks

Twitter.com/HarlequinBooks

Instagram.com/HarlequinBooks

Pinterest.com/HarlequinBooks

ReaderService.com

**ROMANCE WHEN
YOU NEED IT**

PGENRE2018

Love Harlequin romance?

DISCOVER.

Be the first to find out about promotions,
news and exclusive content!

 Facebook.com/HarlequinBooks

 Twitter.com/HarlequinBooks

 Instagram.com/HarlequinBooks

 Pinterest.com/HarlequinBooks

ReaderService.com

EXPLORE.

Sign up for the Harlequin e-newsletter and
download a free book from any series at
TryHarlequin.com.

CONNECT.

Join our Harlequin community to share
your thoughts and connect with other
romance readers!
Facebook.com/groups/HarlequinConnection

**ROMANCE WHEN
YOU NEED IT**

HSOCIAL2018

Reward the book lover in you!

Earn points on your purchase of new Harlequin books from participating retailers.

Turn your points into **FREE BOOKS** of your choice!

Join for FREE today at **www.HarlequinMyRewards.com.**

Harlequin My Rewards is a free program (no fees) without any commitments or obligations.

MYR18